Helen Cresswell

Bagthorpes Unlimited

being the third part of the
Bagthorpe Saga

Illustrated by Jill Bennett

Puffin Books
in association with Faber & Faber

Puffin Books,
Penguin Books Ltd, Harmondsworth,
Middlesex, England
Penguin Books, 625 Madison Avenue,
New York, New York 10022, U.S.A.
Penguin Books Australia Ltd, Ringwood,
Victoria, Australia
Penguin Books Canada Ltd, 2801 John Street,
Markham, Ontario, Canada L3R 1B4
Penguin Books (N.Z.) Ltd, 182–190 Wairau Road,
Auckland 10, New Zealand

First published by Faber & Faber 1978
Published in Puffin Books 1980
Reprinted 1980 (twice)

Made and printed in Great Britain by
Hazell Watson & Viney Ltd
Aylesbury, Bucks
Set in Linotype Granjon

Puffin Books
Bagthorpes Unlimited

It was humiliating for the Bagthorpe family when the burglar looked through all the treasures he had purloined from their house and dumped the lot in disgust at the end of the garden, but it was worst of all for Grandma Bagthorpe, for the insensitive burglar had even spurned the sacred relics of her malevolent but adored cat, Thomas.

So, summoning the shreds of her injured dignity, she announced, 'I wish to see my children, and my children's children gathered together, so that I can feel my life has not been in vain. I want a Family Reunion.'

This speech produced quite a long silence while everyone digested the horrors of what lay in store. For it meant Uncle Claud Bagthorpe and his family coming to stay. Uncle Claud was harmless enough, though too easily crushed, but Aunt Penelope, always quoting the scriptures, and the two admirably clever children, were not. In fact, *anything* was better than being reunited with them so William, Tess, Rosie and Ordinary Jack knew there was only one course open to them – to drive the 'Dogcollar Brigade' from the house at the earliest opportunity!

As you might expect, knowing the Bagthorpes, the desired end could only be achieved after the most monumental mix-ups and mishaps, all recounted with Helen Cresswell's usual sparkling and outrageously humorous invention. The other books in the Bagthorpe Saga, *Ordinary Jack* and *Absolute Zero*, are also in Puffins, of course, as well as *Up the Pier, The Beachcombers, The Night-Watchmen, The Piemakers* and *The Winter of the Birds.*

To Caroline, with love

Acknowledgements

The lines on page 156 are taken from *The Universe* and *The Little Green Orchard* by Walter De la Mare and are quoted by permission of the Literary Trustees of Walter De la Mare and The Society of Authors as their representative.

The passage from *The Guinness Book of Records* on pages 170–71 is quoted by permission of Guinness Superlatives Limited.

Chapter 1

If one had to pinpoint the event that sent the Bagthorpes plunging into the madness that was to possess them for a whole season, then that event would be the burglary. There were other factors, of course, not least among them the infuriating rise to fame of Zero, Grandma and Daisy. But it was the burglary that really triggered things off.

The man who had come to do the burglary could not, as Mr Bagthorpe pointed out, have been very bright, because he ended up stealing all the wrong things. On the other hand, he stole quite a large quantity of things, and must certainly have filled two, or even more, sacks.

It was Grandma who first discovered the crime. The rest of the family were in the kitchen having breakfast when there came from overhead a series of progressively more agonized shrieks. Everyone immediately stopped eating and arguing, and listened. There came a long, high wail.

'It's Mother!' Mrs Bagthorpe pushed back her chair and turned quite pale.

'It's Mother, all right,' Mr Bagthorpe agreed. 'Pass the toast, William. Sit down, Laura.'

'But she might be ill!' protested Mrs Bagthorpe.

'If she were,' replied her husband, 'she would be in no condition to produce noises of that order.'

'True ...' murmured Mrs Bagthorpe, and sank back into her chair. She did not want to create a scene, partly because these were all too frequent a feature of Bagthorpian life already, and partly because she felt that she should set an example by being calm and sensible at all times. (This was to counteract the effect on the children made by Mr Bagthorpe, who was never calm or sensible.)

'I could go and make Mrs Bagthorpe Senior a nice cup tea,' offered Mrs Fosdyke. She had stopped rattling dishes abruptly when the first shriek came, and was plainly agog.

'There's no need for that,' said Mr Bagthorpe in a tightly controlled voice. He had to control his voice fairly tightly when addressing Mrs Fosdyke, because she drove him, as he frequently told people, to the very limits of his sanity.

'Well, she is *old*,' said Mrs Fosdyke defensively.

'Father is eighty-five,' Mr Bagthorpe told her, 'and a full ten years older. *He* is not shrieking for cups of tea.'

This was true. Grandpa was placidly tapping the top of his second boiled egg with his spoon.

'Oh well!' Mrs Fosdyke shrugged and turned back to the sink, where she set up a considerable rattle.

Jack said, 'I think she's coming. The shrieks are getting nearer.'

He was right. The door was flung open and Grandma stood there in her dressing-gown and slippers, with her hair ravelled and amok. She pointed accusingly at her son, looking for all the world like Grendel's mother rising from the mere.

'Heartless wretch!' she cried. 'Did you not hear your own mother calling?'

'When people cry "Wolf!" as often as you do, Mother,' replied Mr Bagthorpe, calmly buttering his toast, 'they tend eventually to get ignored altogether.'

'Come and sit down, Mother,' said Mrs Bagthorpe soothingly, pulling out a chair. 'You look quite upset.'

'Upset?' Grandma's voice was beginning to rise again. 'I am frantic. I am undone!'

'Whatever by?' cried Mrs Bagthorpe. 'I mean, what is the matter?'

'I have been robbed,' Grandma told her dully. 'I have been robbed of all I hold dearest in the world.'

She did sit down then, quite suddenly, and Jack, at least,

realized that she was perfectly serious. His father, on the other hand, showed no sign of being similarly impressed.

'Someone pinched your photo collection, have they?' he inquired unsympathetically. 'Ha! That'll be the day!'

'They have, they have!' Grandma shrieked.

Jack was impressed by the way she uttered these words. It seemed to him that they had the ring of truth. On the other hand, of course, the very idea that anyone should wish to own Grandma's photographs of Thomas was ludicrous. (Thomas, an ill-favoured and malevolent ginger tom, had been the light of Grandma's life until Uncle Parker had inadvertently run him over in the drive some years previously.)

'Grandma,' Jack began, 'have your photos of Thomas really gone?'

'Oh gone, gone, gone!' she moaned.

'In that case,' said Mr Bagthorpe decisively, 'there is evidently a dangerous lunatic at large. We had better telephone the police and report it.'

'All I had left of Thomas were my memories and those wonderful, living likenesses.' Grandma was off on her own now. 'I never felt I had truly lost him until this moment.'

'I shall go and see for myself,' said Mrs Bagthorpe, and went out. She was back quite soon, and was pale again.

'It's true!' she told them all incredulously, as if hoping to be contradicted. Mr Bagthorpe regarded his offspring with a keen eye.

'You four,' he said, 'come on. Who's got 'em?'

The young Bagthorpes set up an instant and noisy chorus of denial and Grandma waved a hand to quell it. In the ensuing silence she scanned dramatically about her and said at last, with absolute conviction:

'It was an outside job!'

Rosie started to giggle and Tess choked into her coffee. Grandma was hooked on television police programmes and was always coming out with this kind of jargon. She had once confided to the Head of Rosie's school that Grandpa had 'done time'. (This was for being a Conscientious Objector, though Grandma did not say so.) On one memorable occasion she had prefaced her reading of the Second Lesson in church by clasping the Bible and swearing to 'tell the truth, the whole truth, and nothing but the truth!' At the end of the Lesson she had slammed the Bible shut in a cloud of dust and cried aggressively 'So help me God!', glaring about the congregation as if daring anyone to stand up and cross-examine.

'There may be other things missing!' Mrs Bagthorpe was becoming agitated. She did yoga daily to try to keep calm, but it did not seem to work all that well. On the other hand, her children often speculated about what she would be like if she did *not* do yoga.

'If there are other things missing, they will certainly not be missed,' Mr Bagthorpe told her. 'Not if this burglar's taste runs to things like photos of that damned cat.'

'Henry!' Mrs Bagthorpe was now quivering. 'Do try to be serious. Our home has been broken into during the night. We must investigate.'

'Come on!' William moved for the door. 'What about my radio equipment?'

'I shall go and 'ave a look in the sitting-room, Mrs Bagthorpe,' volunteered Mrs Fosdyke, arming herself with a brush. She went out. Grandma lifted her head.

'There's no need,' she said mournfully. 'I *know* what has been taken.'

'You *know*?' repeated Mrs Bagthorpe. 'How can you possibly, dear?'

'I have a list,' replied Grandma incomprehensively.

'Left a list, has he?' Mr Bagthorpe said. 'First time I've ever known *that*. Thorough, this burglar fellow.'

Grandma turned her gaze on her son.

'*I* made the list, Henry,' she told him.

'You mean you've been up since the crack of dawn writing down all that's been taken?' asked Tess admiringly.

'Golly Grandma!' exclaimed Rosie.

Grandma shook her head, and one or two hairpins slipped and fell with a kind of melancholy, like the last leaves of the year.

'You don't understand,' she said. 'I made the list *before* the burglary.'

'Oh my God!' Mr Bagthorpe pushed back his chair. 'We haven't another prophet* on our hands, for heaven's sake! You're *rambling*, Mother. Pull yourself together.'

'I want a cup of hot sweet tea,' Grandma said. 'I am suffering from shock. Oh Thomas!'

She took a maddeningly long time to sip the tea Mrs Bagthorpe leapt to supply, and during this hiatus Mrs Fosdyke reappeared. She positively ran into the room in her best hedgehog manner.

'Oh – oh – there's the blue teapot gone off the sideboard!' she cried, 'and the Portraits off of the walls!'

'*My* Portraits!' Rosie squealed and rushed out to see for herself.

Portraits were one of the Strings to Rosie's Bow (the others being the violin, Mental Arithmetic and Photography, including Keeping Records). The previous year she had painted Birthday Portraits of both herself and Grandma which Mrs

* See *Ordinary Jack*.

Bagthorpe had judged good enough to be framed and hung in the sitting-room.

'Thank goodness you weren't in there, old chap,' Jack said sotto voce to Zero, who was slumped by him as he usually was at breakfast. (He was referring to Zero's Portrait, not to Zero himself.) As it happened his relief was to be short-lived.

'There is no need for people to keep running about the house,' proclaimed Grandma dismally. 'We already know the worst. The man obviously followed my list to the letter.'

Here she held up a sheet of notepaper, covered on both sides in her own neat, slanting hand.

'Give that to me,' ordered Mr Bagthorpe, snatching it from her. Half-way down the first page he yelled, 'My God! My scripts!' and ran from the room.

Grandma then tried to explain to those left in the kitchen what had happened.

It appeared that several weeks previously she had read an article about burglary and precautions that might be taken against it. Somebody interviewed had passed on what had seemed to Grandma like a useful tip. Whenever he went away, this man said, he always left on the kitchen table a letter for any burglar who might come, and twenty pounds in used five pound notes. The letter said: 'There is nothing of any real value in this house, so please do not ransack it. Please take the twenty pounds with my compliments.'

Apparently a burglar had come once, and this strategy had worked. The burglar even scrawled 'Thanks' on the bottom of the letter. It was, this man explained, much better to lose twenty pounds in this tidy way than to come back home and find the entire house turned upside down and all sorts of things missing.

The logic of this had appealed to Grandma. Being Grandma, however, she had not been able to resist embroidering on the idea. Also, she had been reluctant to part with twenty pounds, particularly as the house was not her own, but her son's. What she had therefore done was write a letter to any intending burglar, listing all the items she would prefer him not to steal, but giving him a more or less open invitation to take anything else in the house. She left the letter every night on her dressing table before retiring. This would not have been so bad had she not, with uncharacteristic altruism, made a bid to ensure the safety of other people's most prized possessions as well.

'It did seem selfish,' she said, 'simply to look after my own.'

What had started off as a brief note of her own treasures – her photographs of Thomas and of her children and grandchildren (in that order), and her current piece of tapestry – had become a full-scale inventory of other people's as well. The note ran as follows:

Dear Burglar,

I am leaving this note in the hope that you will read it carefully and consider what it says. There are things in this house that I would particularly like you not to take.

1. All photographs in this room, especially those of Thomas.
2. The tapestry and workbox on the chest of drawers.
3. The blue teapot on the sideboard in the sitting-room.
4. The pile of comics and portrait of a dog in the room second on the left.
5. Any scripts in the study downstairs especially if handwritten.
6. The Portraits in the sitting-room.
7. All correspondence in the large file marked PROBLEMS on the desk, bedroom third on right.
8. The hearing aid on the bedside table next door.

9. Notebook labelled 'Hams: Friends and Anonymous' on top of the cupboard 1st bedroom on left second floor.
10. Black belt hanging on wall bedroom end of passage.

If you leave them, and just take anything else, I shall be most grateful.

Yours faithfully
Grace Bagthorpe (Mrs)

When Mr Bagthorpe finally read this missive he gave it out that in his opinion any burglar who had been influenced by these instructions was either stark mad or satanically clever, and that in either case he was dangerous, and should not be at large.

At this, Mrs Fosdyke, who had been fidgeting about in the hall itching to dial 999 pounced towards the telephone, but was prevented by Mr Bagthorpe, who nimbly interposed himself between her and the instrument.

'Wait!' he commanded.

He looked about at the other Bagthorpes, who had been darting about the house confirming their losses and had now reassembled in varying degrees of upset ranging from cold fury (William) to near hysteria (Mrs Bagthorpe).

'We have to think this thing through,' he told them. 'So we call the police. So they send out a squad car with a couple of mutton-brained half-baked police cadets, and what do we report? That we have been robbed of priceless Van Dycks (this aimed at Rosie), and a length of black cotton (this at Tess), and a pile of *comics*, for God's sake?'

'But my letters!' moaned his wife.

'To hell with your letters!' ground Mr Bagthorpe. 'If anything's priceless and beyond replacement, it's my scripts!'

'But – oh!' Mrs Bagthorpe's hand flew to her mouth in a theatrical gesture. 'Henry – I saw – quick – a man! Out there!'

She gestured towards the window of the burned-out dining-room, visible from the hall through the half-open door.

Mr Bagthorpe made for the front door, flung it open and disappeared.

'Quickly!'

Unceremoniously Mrs Bagthorpe pushed Mrs Fosdyke aside and seized the telephone. She dialled rapidly, three digits.

'Hello? Hello? Police! Oh, quickly! A burglary – Unicorn House, Passingham. Quick – and possible blackmail! Oh – oh!'

She rapidly replaced the receiver as Mr Bagthorpe re-entered, breathing heavily.

'Gone!' he said disgustedly. 'Are you *sure* you saw someone?'

Mrs Bagthorpe evaded this question by saying with an efficient air:

'Now, I want everyone to go away and write down what is missing.'

'We've got Mother's list, haven't we?' said her husband bitterly.

'Certainly,' she replied. 'But the burglar may have used his own initiative and taken something that was *not* on the list.'

'I don't see how sitting round and making lists is going to get my scripts back,' he told her.

'But it may assist the police in their inquiries,' she replied. She then looked him bravely in the eye and said, 'I have called the police, Henry.'

'You've – ? Oh, I see. Very clever. If I had suffered a coronary chasing a non-existent burglar there would have been, I hope, some qualms of conscience. I see. My own helpmeet!'

He shook his head wearily and went into his study, closing the door behind him.

The police arrived very promptly. They had been informed that the telephone call reporting the crime had been cut short and that the caller was possibly being attacked. Mrs Bagthorpe was slightly flustered by this, but passed the whole thing off by saying how comforting it was to know that in the event of an emergency the police could be summoned with such speed.

'Now then,' said one of them inevitably at last. 'What seems to be the nature of the problem?'

Telling the police about the crime was as embarrassing as Mr Bagthorpe had said it would be. It took a very long time, because at first they quite genuinely did not know what the Bagthorpes were talking about. They were given Grandma's letter, and were rendered blank by it. At length one of them, after a prolonged study of the list, asked intelligently:

'These portraits – valuable, are they?'

'Yes!' said Rosie, and 'No!' chorused most of the rest simultaneously.

'Antiques, were they?'

'No they were *not*!' squealed Rosie indignantly. 'I'm only nine, and I only *did* them last year.'

'You? You painted them?'

'It's one of the Strings to her Bow,' Tess explained.

'Oh,' said the policeman wisely, 'I see.'

He did not, of course. He did not really see anything. Nor did his colleague. When Grandma looked as if she were going to start explaining her strategy for the third time, Mrs Bagthorpe became restive.

'The really important matter, officer,' she interrupted, 'is item seven. The letters.'

'Ah, the letters,' said the policeman. 'Valuable, were they?'

He seemed bent on finding something valuable, which at least, Jack supposed, would make some kind of sense of the situation.

'Not valuable,' replied Mrs Bagthorpe. 'Potential dynamite.'

Jack saw the younger policeman write 'dynamite' in his notebook, and underline it.

'Those letters,' Mrs Bagthorpe went on, 'are a potential source of blackmail. If they fall into the wrong hands, not one person will be blackmailed, or two, or three, but hundreds.'

There followed another digression while Mrs Bagthorpe explained about her *alter persona* as Stella Bright, who ran a Problem Page in a woman's Monthly.

'You can have no idea of the range of human weakness and corruption revealed in the letters I receive,' she told the bewildered policemen. 'People lay bare their inmost souls.'

'Crimes, are there?' inquired the senior officer, sounding interested.

'There are,' she replied with dignity, 'but not crimes that you need concern yourself with, officer. Those letters are private and sacrosanct. I am bound by an inviolable oath of secrecy. If those letters fall into your hands, I shall want your word of honour that you will not tamper with them, but return them intact and unread.'

'I think they ought to swear,' put in Grandma now. She had perked up considerably since the police arrived. 'I'll fetch the Bible, and they can swear.'

She accordingly nipped out and returned with not only a Bible but Mr Bagthorpe as well. He nodded curtly at the policemen.

'I dissociate myself entirely from this matter,' he told them without preliminaries.

'Naturally, sir,' replied the senior of the two. 'A most unfortunate train of circumstances, as I see it.'

'Unfortunate?' echoed Mr Bagthorpe. 'Train of circumstances? The whole thing is a diabolical welter of lunacy. You've never come across a case like it, I don't suppose?'

They agreed warmly that they certainly had not, and implied that this was something for which they were grateful.

'Though evidently the old lady thought she was being helpful,' one of them misguidedly remarked.

'Old lady?' shrieked Grandma, and 'Helpful?' yelled her son, more or less simultaneously.

'That little plot of hers has been helpful to no one on the face of this earth,' went on Mr Bagthorpe. 'It has not even been helpful to the *burglar*, for God's sake. Someone, somewhere, is cursing it as loud and as long as I am.'

'He certainly doesn't seem to have made much of a haul, sir,' agreed the senior policeman. 'And I suppose that is something to be thankful for.'

At this the entire Bagthorpe family, and especially Mr Bagthorpe, rounded on the pair of them.

'You seem,' Mr Bagthorpe told them coldly, 'to have missed the entire point. What has been taken may not be of much value to the common or garden burglar, but is of inestimable value to ourselves and, in my own case, the nation.'

He then went on to tell them about his two latest scripts. Fortunately, all the others had been typed in duplicate (he had taken to doing this after a raid on his study by Daisy Parker, aged four, who had posted one of his scripts off to a fictitious address, never to return).

At the same time Grandma renewed her lamentations for

her photographs of Thomas and Mrs Bagthorpe was quite desperately trying to get over to somebody the importance of Stella Bright's letters being retrieved. The younger Bagthorpes were themselves in a fair lather.

'It was shocking to hear 'em,' Mrs Fosdyke later confided to her cronies in The Fiddler's Arms. 'I didn't hardly know where to put myself. What them policemen must've thought I don't know. It's a wonder they didn't arrest the lot of 'em for madness.'

The police certainly left quite quickly after this, saying that they would return later for full statements.

'Any statement I make,' said Mr Bagthorpe, 'will be unprintable. And let's hope to God this doesn't get into the papers.'

Chapter 2

The Bagthorpe Robbery did, of course, get into the papers. The *Aysham Gazette*, which Mr Bagthorpe had frequently taken to task in the past, featured it prominently. The family had been forbidden by Mr Bagthorpe to speak to the Press or allow their photographs to be taken, but certain of them, notably Grandma, had been unable to resist the temptation. When, however, she saw the caption above her picture, which read OLD AGE PENSIONER MOURNS TREASURED RELICS she much regretted this. Mr Bagthorpe, on the other hand, could scarcely conceal his delight. Grandma, he went round saying, had become drunk with the heady wine of publicity, and was now draining its bitter dregs. (Grandma got a lot of TV publicity in advertisements for soap and toothpaste, as a result of her success in the recent Bagthorpian Competition Entering craze.)*

'I shall sue them,' she declared. 'Old Age Pensioner indeed!'

'Unfortunately, Mother,' Mr Bagthorpe told her, 'you *are* an Old Age Pensioner, and there are no grounds whatever for libel. It is time you learned to accept your age gracefully.'

'I am *technically* an Old Age Pensioner,' she returned frigidly, 'and it is like you, Henry, to reduce everything to its lowest common denominator. Nobody ever calls Sybil Thorndyke an Old Age Pensioner, or the Queen Mother.'

The newspaper report did nothing to enhance the image

* See *Absolute Zero*.

of any of the Bagthorpes, and had clearly been written by a reporter to whom Mr Bagthorpe had been particularly rude in the past.

'We emerge,' he said gloomily, 'as buffoons.'

The account of Grandma's strategy as explained by herself, followed by a photocopy of the letter she had written to the burglar, certainly made an original story. One of the first people to offer commiserations was Uncle Parker.

Although his wife, Celia, was Mr Bagthorpe's sister, and although the Parkers lived only just over a mile away from Unicorn House, they had not been told of the burglary. This had been on Mr Bagthorpe's express instructions. He and Uncle Parker lived in a perpetual state of feud. Uncle Parker always seemed to wear a faintly amused expression and Mr Bagthorpe felt that he could not bear it if his brother-in-law were to come around wearing that expression at the present time. Mr Bagthorpe was spending most of his time holed up in his study, partly trying feverishly to recall the better lines from the stolen scripts, and partly to keep out of the way of the police, who maddened him so much that he was frightened he might attack them.

Uncle Parker, then, accompanied by Aunt Celia and Daisy, came roaring up the drive early on the morning following the burglary. Mr Bagthorpe heard them, all right – nobody could miss the kind of noise Uncle Parker always made – but he sat tight, and speculated whether the police could arrest Uncle Parker for dangerous driving in a drive.

The rest of the Bagthorpe ménage was in the kitchen with two different policemen, making final statements. (This was the third pair of policemen who had called. None of them seemed to want to make more than one visit. 'Someone new might throw a different light on the case' they told their superiors, and on this occasion the sergeant had come to see for himself.)

'Hallo, there!' called Uncle Parker and entered the kitchen with an air of pronounced jauntiness which he dropped as soon as he perceived that Mr Bagthorpe was not present to be infuriated by it.

'Bad *luck*, Laura,' he said to Mrs Bagthorpe sympathetically, dropping a kiss on her head.

'Oh Laura – darling . . .' moaned Aunt Celia, who was easily made distraught by catastrophes even when they were outside her own immediate sphere. She was not really of this world even under normal circumstances, and spent much of her time writing poetry or throwing pots, or else thinking about these activities. When she did occasionally surface into everyday reality, it was always a shock to her system.

Her five-year-old daughter, on the other hand, was always on the ball. Aunt Celia claimed that Daisy took after herself and was creative, but nobody else could see this, not even Grandma, who was Daisy's ally, and liked to think Daisy took after *her*.

'That infant,' Mr Bagthorpe was fond of saying, 'is the only person I know who can be destructively creative. And there is no such thing as destructive creativity.'

'Oh Grandma Bag!' squealed Daisy, rushing to embrace her. 'Mummy says there's been some mazic and it's mazicked your Thomases away!'

The rest of the Bagthorpes looked askance at this exposition of their plight, and Uncle Parker explained sotto voce that Aunt Celia had thought it best for the word 'burglar' not to be used in Daisy's presence. She had this delusion that Daisy was highly strung and sensitive, though even those of the Bagthorpes who quite liked Daisy knew it to be a myth. She had, they were aware, marked criminal tendencies of her own, and had in her time been a notable pyromaniac.*

Aunt Celia beckoned to the policemen who got up and went to her, looking bewildered but pleased. (Aunt Celia was very beautiful and ethereal-looking, and not so entirely removed from reality that she was not able to make use of her ornamental value when this was expedient.) She whispered to the policemen for a minute or two and they nodded sympathetically. The family soon found out what Aunt Celia had been whispering, because for the rest of the interview the policemen, albeit sheepishly, referred to the burglar as 'the magician'. Fortunately, the proceedings were almost at an end.

'If we do get any kind of lead on the – er – magician involved,' the senior policeman promised, 'we shall immediately let you know. But this particular kind of bur – er – magic – is extremely difficult, insomuch as the property – er– magicked away – is unlikely to be passed through any of our known channels.'

'Such a worry, though. . . .' Mrs Bagthorpe during the last twenty-four hours had cast her yoga to the winds and not behaved by any means as coolly as Stella Bright would doubtless have advised. 'We must only hope this – magician – does not have a contact who is interested in the other branch of magic – you know – b-l-a-c-k-m-a-i-l.'

She spelled out this last word in the vain hope of foxing Daisy, but that precocious child immediately pricked up her ears and cried:

'Black what? Black what, Auntie Bag?'

'Black beetles, Daisy,' said Uncle Parker with commend-

* See *Ordinary Jack*.

able promptness. 'To do spells with.'

'What kind of spells?' persisted Daisy, interested. One could almost see her mental processes at work. *She* intended to go into magic, if possible.

'The kind that magics off inquisitive small girls,' said William, who was no admirer of Daisy's.

Daisy squealed and Aunt Celia cast a reproachful look at William. Even the policeman looked disapproving and as if about to warn him.

At this juncture Mr Bagthorpe entered.

'Just off?' he asked the police, in a way that definitely implied that they had better be. He went over and poured himself a coffee, ignoring the Parkers.

'Yes, sir. Oh – and one last thing. The dog.'

Jack's heart beat fast. He had been waiting for this.

'Deaf, is he?' the policeman asked him sympathetically.

'Well, no . . .' Jack began. His father whipped round.

'Deaf?' he echoed. 'Deaf, daft, useless – you name it!'

'Well, yes, sir. We've seen the advertisements. My two kids are quite fans of his, as a matter of fact. Got the badges and posters and the lot. Does that advert very well, we think.'*

He was referring to the television commercial starring Zero made by BURIED BONES dog food. In this, Zero just acted in his usual bewildered way, and by doing so had become the idol of millions. It was not a topic Mr Bagthorpe liked to have touched on even under normal circumstances, and in the present context the reference to it acted like the proverbial red rag.

'Could there have been another dog in England,' he asked the police, 'who would have in the first place been spending the night guarding a pile of comics, and in the second

* See *Absolute Zero.*

allowed a burglar to step over him and remove them? There's no proof, of course, but it's more than probable the animal *licked* him!'

'*Magician*, dear,' Mrs Bagthorpe said, trying to catch her husband's eye.

'Magician?' he repeated. 'What in the name of reason are you burbling about?'

'The magician who came and magicked our things away,' said Mrs Bagthorpe very slowly and distinctly, while making little flicking movements of her eyes in Daisy's direction. She looked and sounded slightly mad.

'*Daisy* is quite excited about the *magician*,' Mrs Bagthorpe added desperately. Her point evidently got through.

'Oh my God!' exclaimed Mr Bagthorpe in disgust. 'All right, so the accursed hound licked the *magician*. The point is, any other dog would have bitten him.'

'Zero was tired last night,' Jack said defensively. 'He'd been rabbiting.'

'Ha!' Mr Bagthorpe let out one of his sardonic laughs. 'Would you believe,' he asked the police, 'that on one occasion I saw that mutton-headed hound being pursued across a field *by* a rabbit?'

'Well, sir...' The policeman looked dubious. 'That is stretching it a bit...'

'*I* don't believe it,' said Jack stoutly. 'I think you imagined it, Father.'

'You do, after all, have a wonderful imagination, Henry,' put in Mrs Bagthorpe, hoping to pour oil on troubled waters. Her son was no real match for her husband in a verbal encounter. Nobody was, for that matter, except perhaps Grandma and Uncle Parker.

'Of course I do!' Mr Bagthorpe snapped ungratefully. 'And I also have perfectly good eyesight. Kindly allow me to be the judge of what I saw and did not saw – I mean see.'

'Well, sir –' the sergeant moved towards the door – 'we'd best be off and pursue our inquiries.'

'You do that,' Mr Bagthorpe told him.

The police left, and Jack followed them with Zero in case Mr Bagthorpe renewed his attack. Zero had never had very much self-confidence and it was constantly being shaken by Mr Bagthorpe's slights and jeers, which Jack was convinced Zero understood. Zero's ears drooped when he felt sad and undermined, and Jack would give him long pep talks to try to get them up again. Even now that Zero was a household word and had a fan club, his position in the family had not really altered.

'Don't take any notice, old chap,' Jack told Zero as they turned the corner of the house and made down the garden towards the meadow beyond. 'He's just jealous.'

Mr Bagthorpe wrote scripts for television and most weeks Zero had more screen time than he did. Also, Mr Bagthorpe did not have a fan club or have life-sized posters made of him.

It was late March; wind and sun blew over the meadow in giant waves, and Jack raced the clouds in the direction of the village, stopping every now and then to throw something for Zero to 'Fetch'. Every time Zero Fetched, Jack patted and praised him, and after a while the ears seemed to pick up a little. This made Jack himself feel better.

Jack's own confidence was never very high. He was the sole ordinary person (with the exception of Grandpa, who was deaf and did not really notice) in a family of what were certainly eccentrics, if not, as they themselves claimed, geniuses. They all had several fields in which they excelled, and these were known, in a phrase coined by Mrs Bagthorpe, as

Strings to their Bows. William, for instance, had four Strings to his Bow – electronics, mathematics, tennis and playing on the drums. Tess also had four, including reading Voltaire in the original and a Black Belt in Judo, and even Rosie, who was only nine, had three definite and one almost.

Jack, on the other hand, had none. He had once, with Uncle Parker's connivance, made a bid to convince his family that he was endowed with supernatural power and was, amongst other things, a Prophet.* This scheme had started off well enough, but ended by his being found out in a dramatic denouement at Rosie's Birthday Party. The rest of the Bagthorpes did not exactly despise Jack for his lack of achievement, but they did tend to treat him in a patronizing way. They did not see him as an equal.

Jack's present motive in going to the village was firstly to remove himself and Zero as far as possible from Mr Bagthorpe, and secondly to visit the shop, where Zero would be much patted and praised by anyone who happened to be in there. Nobody had ever patted and praised Zero before the BURIED BONES commercial, but now everybody did it.

Jack was not disappointed. There were several people in the shop, including one of Mrs Fosdyke's special cronies, Mrs Pye. All transactions came to a standstill while Zero was thoroughly patted and favourably commented on. Mrs Pye herself had done a complete about-turn in her estimation of Zero, and now kept proclaiming, almost belligerently:

'I should like anyone to show me another dog that could've made a film like this dog did.'

Before, she used to say that Zero had great, dirty paws, and was stupid.

Unfortunately, two of the people present in the shop were a photographer and a reporter from the *Aysham Gazette*,

* See *Ordinary Jack*.

who had learned from the police that the dog involved in the Bagthorpe Burglary was the nationwide favourite starring in the BURIED BONES commercial. Jack did not know this, because they did not introduce themselves. The photographer purchased a tin of tobacco as a front for his being in the shop, and then followed Jack and Zero out and took a photograph of Zero.

Jack was used by now to complete strangers coming up and taking photographs of Zero, and did not realize that anything untoward was afoot until the reporter caught up and fell into step beside him. He introduced himself and began to ask questions about the part Zero had played in the Burglary.

'Did he sound the alarm?' he asked hopefully, already visualizing his headline: BURIED BONES BAGTHORPE BEATS BURGLAR.

'Not exactly,' replied Jack truthfully. 'He would have done, normally, but he was worn out. He'd been rabbiting all day.'

'Caught many, did he?' asked the reporter, mentally changing his headline and reluctantly realizing he would have to relinquish the alliteration.

'He doesn't *try* to catch them,' replied Jack with dignity. 'He just chases them. He's Anti Blood Sports.'

He gradually found himself telling the reporter where Zero had been during the fateful night and what he had been doing. Zero had been so feted since his BURIED BONES commercial that it simply did not occur to Jack that Zero could ever receive any adverse publicity.

He found his mistake the following morning, when he was shown the front page of the *Aysham Gazette*, which featured a photograph of Zero trying to keep his balance while scratching his right ear with his right paw, under a headline that read:

BURIED BONES BAGTHORPE BUNGLES BURGLARY

Jack's own fury was matched only by Mr Bagthorpe's. The latter had just received a telephone call from Uncle Parker congratulating him on the story and implying that he, Mr Bagthorpe, had been responsible for it.

'Let's face it, if you're a writer, any publicity is good publicity, eh, Henry?' he had said just before Mr Bagthorpe slammed down the receiver.

'And describing that pudding-footed disaster as a Bagthorpe,' he fumed. 'As if I'd spawned the thing. I'll sue!'

Grandma, seeing her chance of revenge, picked up her cue neatly.

'He is a part of this household,' she told him, 'and so quite legitimately described as a Bagthorpe. There are no grounds whatever for libel. You should learn to take yourself less seriously, Henry.'

Jack, following his usual evasive strategy, took Zero for a walk in the meadow, but later this proved to have been a mistake.

Just as the Bagthorpes were finishing lunch that day the original pair of policemen knocked on the door. (The local constabulary had evidently run out of available manpower.) They had found, they said, with the aid of a trained Alsatian dog, the missing property.

The noisy and exultant reactions to this intelligence were cut short when the Bagthorpes came to understand the exact nature of the discovery. All the missing items had been found in a large sack dumped by the wicket gate that led from the garden into the meadow. Everything was intact, except that all the Portraits and photographs had been taken from their frames and were bundled up loosely. It was obvious, the policemen said, that the burglar had expected to find large sums of money secreted behind them. Never in their experience, they said, had any burglar so promptly returned stolen goods, and certainly never before had the thief left a note similar to the one attached by a safety pin to the top of the sack.

It read:

I WOLD HAVE BURNED THIS LOT OF RUBISH BUT THE MISSUS SED IT WOLD CLOG THE GRATE. IT WAS A DIRTY TRICK TO STOOP TO.
YOURS FAITHFULLY – DISGUSTED

This message was printed in full in the following day's *Aysham Gazette*, together with a humiliating account of where and how it had been found. On reading it, Mr Bagthorpe said:

'That does it. We shall all have to leave the district. And why in the name of all that's wonderful did not that numb-nosed hound of yours sniff it out when he went past?'

Jack and Zero went for another walk.

Chapter 3

The Burglary, then, had a very unsettling effect on the Bagthorpes. One might have thought that, having recovered the stolen property intact against all likelihood, they would have thought themselves lucky. They did not – or, at least, not for very long.

The *Aysham Gazette* had evidently thought the story of the Bagthorpe Burglary too good to keep to themselves and had passed it on to a national news agency. The result was that practically every national daily covered it the following day, in each case giving the job of writing it up to the humorist on their staff. When Mr Bagthorpe said that the family was now the laughing stock of England, he was hardly exaggerating.

To be robbed of one's most valued possessions is a traumatic experience and one that would normally excite sympathy. But to have these same valued possessions dumped straight back at the bottom of one's garden with a dismissive note from the burglar, is another thing again.

All the Bagthorpes found themselves shunning contact with other people because they could not endure the kind of remarks that were constantly being made to them. Mrs Fosdyke, of course, was unavoidable, and had to be put up with. Mr Bagthorpe, who was always trying to get rid of her, thought that now was the moment to sack her, but his wife would not hear of it.

'She is the oil that makes the wheels of this household

turn,' she said, 'and her leaving would mean the end of Stella Bright.'

As if to rub salt in the wound, the BURIED BONES people rang up to say how enchanted they were by all the publicity Zero had had, and asking if Mr Bagthorpe had arranged it all. They said they wanted to make another commercial featuring Zero.

'This would be along the same lines as the first,' they explained, 'except that this time we would show him sleeping by a pile of comics, and instead of saying "Zero can't even act" we should say "Zero can't even catch a burglar when he is right under his nose" . . .'

Jack thought his father overreacted to this suggestion.

'I don't see why you should mind,' he protested. 'If Zero and me don't mind, I don't see why you should. And after all, it's his career.'

The Burglary had a particularly bad effect on Grandma. It seemed to the others that it was she who had engineered the whole thing and so she received scant sympathy.

'Next time you leave a note for an intruder,' Mr Bagthorpe told her, 'suggest he kidnaps you.'

She spent hours in her room carefully putting the photographs of Thomas back in their frames and rearranging them. For two days she had all her meals sent up on a tray, and on the third she emerged, managing to look quite frail and sad.

'I have decided,' she announced, during the course of an unusually silent breakfast, 'that I wish to gather my family about me.'

They glanced at her but went on eating.

'The events of the past few days,' she continued, in what was evidently a well rehearsed speech, 'have brought home to me the uncertainties of human existence. I have realized on what a slender thread our happiness depends.'

She paused.

'I think we have all realized that, Mother,' said Mr Bagthorpe through a mouthful of toast, 'and some of us, of course, have realized it for years.'

'"The search for happiness is one of the chief sources of unhappiness" – George Bernard Shaw,' offered Tess.

She was favoured by a cold stare from Mr Bagthorpe, who could never, to save his life, come up with an apt quotation.

'Anonymous from Grimsby reckons the whole of civilization hangs by a thread,' William said. 'He reckons there's an Alien Intelligence out there, and its signals are getting stronger.'

This contribution to the general angst cut no ice with the rest of the family.

'We don't much care what an anonymous radio ham from Grimsby says,' Tess told him, 'even if we believed in his existence, which some of us don't.'

'Nobody is listening to me at all,' complained Grandma, with justification. 'I am trying to say something important.'

'You were trying to say you wanted to gather your family about you,' Mrs Bagthorpe said helpfully. 'We are your family, Mother, and we *are* around you.'

'I feel the need to gather my *whole* family about me,' Grandma said. 'I wish to see my children, and my children's children gathered together, so that I can feel my life has not been in vain. I want a Family Reunion.'

This speech produced quite a long silence.

'What she is really saying,' Mr Bagthorpe told the rest of the table at length, 'is that she wants Claud and his sainted tribe, though why, I am at a loss to imagine. If you want to see Claud, Mother, you go and see him. Leave the rest of us out of it.'

Grandma turned a piteous gaze on him.

'I don't think you understand, Henry,' she said. 'I want my whole brood about me. And I am an old lady,' she added, with uncharacteristic honesty, 'and I think my wishes ought to be respected.'

Mrs Bagthorpe looked worried at this.

'Are you sure you have really thought about it,' she asked, 'and all it would entail?'

'Of course she hasn't!' snapped Mr Bagthorpe. 'She would be driven out of her mind by that bunch of latter-day saints before any of us. She's probably forgotten that Penelope never stops quoting the scriptures!'

'A familiarity with the scriptures is not a vice, Henry,' said Grandma piously.

'Possibly not,' he returned. 'But the non-stop evoking of them *is*.'

He was, of course, exaggerating, but the rest of the family were by and large with him on this score. Uncle Claud himself was inoffensive enough. If he irritated anyone, it was Grandma herself, because she liked people to show some fight. There was nothing Grandma enjoyed more than an all-out row, and Claud was hopeless in this respect. He was very mild and absentminded and took after Grandpa. He was a parson, although, as Mr Bagthorpe was fond of saying, one would have thought it was Aunt Penelope who had taken Holy Orders.

'She certainly *acts* as if she were under Holy Orders,' he said, 'and so far as I am concerned, anyone who thinks that sherry is something you use to flavour a trifle with, is a stranger in my house.'

On previous visits from the Dogcollar Brigade, as he called them, Mr Bagthorpe had been driven to taking his whiskies at The Fiddler's Arms. He preferred, he said, to knock them back under the gimlet eyes of Mrs Fosdyke and Co., than to endure Aunt Penelope's condemnatory stare.

'And when she's around,' he stated, 'I *need* to drink.'

The young Bagthorpes were not much more enthusiastic about the proposed Reunion. Their Dogcollar cousins, Esther aged seven and Luke aged eleven, were prim and unsmiling and, what was worse, extremely clever. They did not call their accomplishments Strings to Bows, and boast shamelessly about them. They were merely infuriatingly clever, and somehow managed to let people know this without actually seeming to try. Esther, moreover, told tales.

'I don't think I ask very much of life,' Grandma now went on. 'I try not to trouble people.'

'It would, of course, entail a lot of extra work,' said Mrs Bagthorpe.

At this point Mrs Fosdyke chipped in.

'Oh, don't mind me, Mrs Bagthorpe,' she said. 'Not the least trouble, the Reverend gentleman and his lady. And as for their children – 'elpfulness itself. Such lovely manners.'

For this unsolicited testimonial she was rewarded by murderous glares from the younger Bagthorpes and from Mr Bagthorpe himself. The latter did not mind the implied criticism of his own offspring, though he had not particularly cared for the way she had emphasized the word 'gentleman'. What he could not stand was Mrs Fosdyke's continually butting in on conversations. This was one of the worst side effects of having a burnt out dining-room,* and having to eat every meal in the kitchen. Mrs Fosdyke was either listening, banging and rattling pots, or else putting her spoke in.

* See *Absolute Zero.*

'There you are!' cried Grandma triumphantly. 'How very kind of you, Mrs Fosdyke. You see, Laura. It is no trouble at all.'

Grandma's grasp of psychology must have been slipping or she would not have made the mistake of enlisting Mrs Fosdyke as an ally. Nothing could have been better calculated to drive Mr Bagthorpe's heels more firmly in.

'I think it is nervous wear and tear Laura was alluding to, Mother,' he said coldly. 'Not mere domestic chores. Those of us who are of a sensitive disposition, and engaged in wrestling with serious creative work, are easily thrown off balance by disruptive elements. I personally do not believe I could finish my current script while being constantly bombarded by scriptures and texts. I think I would lose my sanity.'

'Oh dear!' Mrs Bagthorpe seemed easily to be able to deal with other people's Problems in the persona of Stella Bright, but was invariably thrown by the Problems that cropped up all too often on her own domestic front. Whenever Mr Bagthorpe pointed this out, she would reply that it was all a matter of perspective, and that in order to view a Problem clearly it was necessary to stand back from it. Once Mr Bagthorpe had written to Stella Bright on a borrowed typewriter, and in his letter had outlined the precise Problem that was currently confronting the Bagthorpe household. To his delight, Stella Bright had replied confirming exactly his own viewpoint in the matter. He had triumphantly waved his reply under Mrs Bagthorpe's nose, and had naturally got his own way. For months after this, whenever he and his wife had a difference of opinion, he would gibe 'What price Stella Bright?' and invariably get his own way again.

'Shall I write to Claud?' Grandma asked, ignoring her son's outburst, 'or will you, Laura?' – thus neatly converting the dilemma into a decision, not as to whether Claud and family should be invited at all, but as to who should do the inviting.

Mr Bagthorpe thereupon pushed back his chair from the table, contenting himself with remarking, 'She's too clever for *you*, Laura,' and left the room. He never fought losing battles through to the end.

It was decided that Mrs Bagthorpe should write and invite the Dogcollar Brigade to stay during the Easter holidays.

'And during that time we shall, of course, have a special party,' she told Grandma, 'a real Family Reunion.'

'Where will you have it, Mrs Bagthorpe?' inquired Mrs Fosdyke, advancing from the sink. 'The dining-room being in no fit state, you won't mind my saying.'

'We can have it in the kitchen,' Tess said. 'If it's good enough for us, it's good enough for them.'

'I don't mind having the only Family Reunion I'm ever likely to have in the kitchen,' said Grandma in a small voice.

'But of *course* we can't have it in here!' cried Mrs Bagthorpe, as Grandma had intended she should. 'We shall push some of the furniture into the hall and move the dining-table into the sitting-room.'

When Mr Bagthorpe was later apprised of these arrangements, he was fatalistic about them.

'The sitting-room will go up in flames,' he predicted, 'and we shall be driven to the last bastion – the kitchen.'

'Or your study,' Tess reminded him.

At the time these arrangements were made, however, he was not present, and things had soon gone too far for him to be able to intervene.

Mrs Fosdyke was wholeheartedly behind the project, and that not merely because she enjoyed catering on a large scale and showing off her considerable culinary skills. She had an unexpected streak of sentimentality, and was much affected by the idea, *per se*, of a Family Reunion.

'I don't think I've ever catered for one of them before,' she confided. 'In fact, I'm sure I ain't. What sort of cake, do you think? I mean, what about the decorations?'

'I leave it entirely to you, Mrs Fosdyke,' said Mrs Bagthorpe diplomatically, 'but I think I must specify that there should be no candles.'

'I should like a message on the cake,' said Grandma wistfully. 'Something like "Forty-Four Years a Mother". Claud would like that.'

'We shall have to see,' Mrs Bagthorpe told her. 'I'm sure we shall think of something apt. Perhaps you could help, darlings?'

She turned hopefully towards her own dispirited brood.

'I'll try,' Rosie promised eventually. 'But there doesn't seem much you can say.'

Mrs Bagthorpe wrote to the Dogcollar Brigade and duly received a letter from Aunt Penelope. She read parts of it out at breakfast.

'The children, bless them, break up on April 1st and we shall be able to come on the 2nd, as you suggest, God willing. We shall be free for three whole weeks.'

At this Mr Bagthorpe looked sharply up from his newspaper.

'Did I hear you aright?' he said. 'How long did you invite them for?'

'I – I don't think I stipulated,' replied his wife weakly.

'Then stipulate,' he told her. 'Fast. Stipulate two days.'

'They do live a hundred and fifty miles away,' she reminded him, 'and that would scarcely be worth their while. In any case, don't you think it would seem rather ungracious to stipulate at this stage? I think we must play things by ear.'

'Do as you like,' he replied. 'But I must tell you that if they stay more than a week, I shall go and stay with Aunt Lucy in Torquay until they have gone.'

Later that day the young Bagthorpes held a meeting. This was something they were not given to. They were essentially loners. They were in competition not only with the world at large, but also with one another. No quarter was given to blood relations. Only rarely did there seem any advantage in combining forces. On this occasion, however, there seemed an emphatic case for it.

They assembled in William's room, which was on the second floor and more out of the way than anyone else's. The reason he had been put up there was because of his amateur radio equipment and his drums. There were usually crackles and whistles or vibrant tattoos or a combination of all these sounds coming from William's room.

'The main business,' said William, who was assuming chairmanship by virtue of being the eldest and on his own territory, 'is to devise a plan for getting the D.B. out of the house as soon after their arrival as possible.'

'We'll have to wait till after the party,' Rosie piped up, 'else Grandma will be disappointed. And I like parties. And I might even do a Family Reunion Portrait, so's I'll have a record. It would be really original, a Family Reunion Portrait.'

No one commented on this suggestion.

'A prime factor in our deliberations,' said Tess, who never used one word where five would do, nor a short one where there was a long one, 'must be to preserve an innocuous front. We must sabotage without seeming to sabotage, we must smile as we plunge the dagger to the hilt.'

'You mean we mustn't let the rest know what we're up to,'

said William, translating. 'You're right. Especially Grandma and Mother. I don't suppose Father would mind.'

'As I view the situation,' Tess went on, 'there are two possible known weaknesses we might exploit to advantage. One is that Esther and Luke have an inordinate fear of the supernatural –'

'Remember that Christmas Father told that ghost story and Esther went into hysterics and drummed her heels and her shoe flew off and hit Grandpa?'

'– the other,' resumed Tess, ignoring the interruption, 'and possibly more fruitful area for exploitation, is the Sainted Aunt's pathological terror of bacteria and microbes.'

'Golly, yes!' agreed Jack after a moment's pause. 'Germs!'

Aunt Penelope had evidently in her impressionable years been well and truly indoctrinated with the postulate: *Cleanliness is next to Godliness.* Mr Bagthorpe, indeed, maintained that she possibly felt the priorities in this statement to be wrong, and what she actually believed was that *Godliness is next to Cleanliness.* He said it was a toss up. He further said that he thought this belief had affected her physical development, in that she had a very long nose with widely flaring and sometimes twitching nostrils.

'All the better to sniff with,' he claimed, and the others felt he might be right about this.

Aunt Penelope's house was festooned with fly-papers and smelled of carbolic. She used a magnifying glass when washing lettuce and scrubbed eggs before she boiled them. Her obsession with invisible microbes was such that she placed all books borrowed from the Public Library in a hot oven for several minutes, to decontaminate them.

'You never know *where* they have been,' she had told Mrs Bagthorpe with a shudder.

Her offspring had told the young Bagthorpes that once she

had forgotten to take the books out, and remembered them only when clouds of acrid smoke had started to issue from the oven. They did not tell this as a joke, but as a matter of plain fact, and were much put out when their cousins had heartlessly rolled about laughing. The books, they said, had been too brown and crisp to return to the library, and had cost Uncle Claud nearly ten pounds to replace.

'That's the best bet,' said William emphatically now. 'Germ warfare it is!'

Chapter 4

Life in the Bagthorpe household often seemed a fair imitation of Bedlam even when things were running relatively smoothly. The week prior to the visit of the Sainted Aunt and her tribe came very close to leaving Bedlam a poor second.

Mrs Bagthorpe and Mrs Fosdyke were deep in domestic preparations that seemed, to Mr Bagthorpe at least, of unnecessary scope and complexity.

'There is no need for all this rearranging of furniture and putting of exotic dishes into deep freeze,' he told his wife. 'The first thing that woman will do on arrival will be to go over the rooms allotted with a fine tooth-comb, looking for fleas. And she will suspect all food of being contaminated whether it has been stored in the deep freeze or a dustbin. That tribe is used, as we know to our cost, to living on minced beef and boiled rice puddings. The rich food you are preparing will upset their stomachs and we shall be accused of poisoning them.'

Mrs Bagthorpe pointed out that were she to dish up mince and rice for a week, Mr Bagthorpe would be the first to up and leave. He evidently took the point, because he quietened down somewhat, and contented himself with going about the house exclaiming, 'Hah! Got you!' and swatting at imaginary insects.

The younger Bagthorpes were deep in their plan to produce as much mould, fungus and decay as possible before

April 2nd. They were also experimenting with William's chemistry set to produce bad smells, and were trying to raise maggots in the airing cupboard.

Luckily, there were two airing cupboards, one being on the top floor and rarely used, and they put most of their things in there, well out of Mrs Fosdyke's way. They had several experiments going at the same time.

'In order to produce fungus,' William told them, 'conditions of warmth and humidity are desirable. The same applies to decomposition of meat, and formation of maggots.'

Several sandwiches encased in polythene bags were laid near the hot-water tank to produce mould, together with three saucers of bread and milk. A metal baking tin, on which were laid slices of beef smuggled from Sunday lunch, was secreted behind a pile of bath towels.

'We shall have to keep a regular check on that,' William warned. 'Maggots move, remember. If old Fozzy comes across maggots moving, she'll quit, sure as eggs. And talking of eggs, I've got a formula.'

He had rung up a school friend and obtained, in exchange for two life-sized posters of Zero, the chemical formula for producing a smell of rotten eggs. He was very confident about this smell.

'Nigel reckons it could kill you,' he told them complacently. 'Not through being poisonous, but through shock.'

'We don't really want anybody to *die* while they're here, do we?' Jack objected. 'I mean, there'd have to be a funeral, and everything. It'd be awful. Let's not bother with the smell.'

'We'll test it out,' William told him. 'If it doesn't make any of us die, I don't see why it should them.'

Rosie and Jack, who were unable to contribute much to the

more technical side of things, were kept busy tracking down spiders, earwigs, slugs and anything else likely to frighten Aunt Penelope into fits.

'We shall place them strategically, at intervals,' William said. 'Little by little we shall turn the screw.'

In addition to all this activity there was an invasion by the Buried Bones people, who wanted to waste no time in making their next commercial.

'We must strike while the iron is hot,' they said, by which they meant while the public could still remember the Bagthorpe Burglary story.

Mr Bagthorpe tried to prevent this, and there was much talk of suing. But the small print of Zero's contract clearly stated that BURIED BONES were to have an option on making a further commercial about Zero 'of a similar nature and at their sole discretion'. Mr Bagthorpe consulted his solicitor, and was told he had no case. The solicitor also laughed while Mr Bagthorpe was explaining.

No one was very pleased about the matter, and even Jack was beginning to have second thoughts about it. It was one thing for a dog not to be able to sniff out BURIED BONES but another for him not to be able to catch burglars.

'Don't you worry about it, old chap,' he told Zero, who was creeping around the house getting nearer and nearer the ground and with his ears plummeting. 'I bet that burglar put an ether pad over your nose. And I bet he had a gun. If you'd woken up and barked, he'd have shot everybody. You saved all our lives. Good old chap. Good old boy!'

None of this really did Zero's morale any good, but the director of the BURIED BONES film seemed to prefer him with his ears down.

'That's his appeal,' he told Jack when he was apologizing about it. 'That's what grabs 'em!'

He said that Zero's performance was even more understated than his first, and would double sales yet again. All the money Zero was earning from his acting was going into a special account, and Jack would reflect that if ever Zero's life really became not worth living, he and Jack could leave home together.

Mr Bagthorpe's anguish had not in fact reached its nadir in the filming of the BURIED BONES commercial, though he might have been forgiven for thinking that it must have. The filming for the first commercial he had missed by being away at a Health Farm, trying to feel his way back into being human again. He had watched both Grandma and Daisy Parker posturing before the film cameras making their commercials, and this had been bad, but to see Zero being given star treatment was more than he could take. When he stood around and sneered, the director told him sharply that some half million people had already sent up for photographs of Zero, that BURIED BONES sales had doubled since his last film, and that all these people could not be wrong.

'In that case,' returned Mr Bagthorpe, 'I shall insert in the Personal Column of *The Times* a formal announcement that I wish to cancel my membership of the human race.'

When Mr Bagthorpe's anguish did reach its nadir the following day, he was driven to the point where he was tempted to cancel his membership of the human race in a more practical way.

'Sometimes suicide is the only possible expression of integrity,' he said.

When Uncle Parker came ripping up the drive around eleven, there was no reason to suppose he had come for any purpose other than to cadge a coffee and make the odd quip about the Burglary. He started off by doing both these things, and in fact did not madden Mr Bagthorpe as much as he had hoped, because Mr Bagthorpe had now had a good idea for a script based on the Burglary, and was quite glad it had happened.

Uncle Parker must have been waiting for an opening before coming to the real point of his visit, and Mr Bagthorpe inevitably ended by giving him one. By the time Uncle Parker had been in the kitchen for half an hour, and was sipping his third cup of coffee and lounging with the air of careless ease he had on the one comfortable chair, Mr Bagthorpe was becoming restive. He himself had work to do. What Uncle Parker did in life in order to maintain his expensive car and elegant lifestyle, no one precisely knew. All that was known was that whatever it was, it took only until ten in the morning, and left Uncle Parker free for the rest of the day to sit around doing crosswords, or tear about in his car putting the fear of God into old and young alike. Mr Bagthorpe, although he referred contemptuously to Uncle Parker as 'that homicidal parasite' and 'that gin-swigging tailor's dummy', was jealous of him.

'I'll get back to my script,' he said pointedly, pushing his cup away. 'I expect you've finished work for the day, Russell?'

'That's right,' Uncle Parker agreed pleasantly. 'The *real* work, anyway.'

'*Real* work?' repeated Mr Bagthorpe. 'Would you like to define that for us?'

'I merely meant that I'm now free to indulge my latest little hobby,' said Uncle Parker mildly. 'Nipping up to London to see this director fellow.'

'Director of the Bank of England?' inquired Mr Bagthorpe.

'*Film* director, Henry,' said Uncle Parker reproachfully.

Mr Bagthorpe stared.

'*You're* not doing commercials?' he demanded. 'Don't tell us you're doing commercials?'

'I told you, Henry – I've taken up this little hobby. You've got to keep your brain active. I've written one or two scripts for television.'

'You've – what?' Mr Bagthorpe's voice was faint and strangled.

Uncle Parker nodded.

'You know – for relaxation.'

Mr Bagthorpe sat down again abruptly.

'Oh Russell!' cried Mrs Bagthorpe. 'You're a dark horse! Did you hear that, Henry? He is writing plays for television.'

'Only for relaxation,' added Uncle Parker again.

Jack winced. His father was being goaded beyond his endurance, even he could see that.

'Relaxation!' Mr Bagthorpe croaked.

Jack felt truly sorry for him. His father was always giving it out that writing scripts was a feat of skill and endurance that ordinary mortals could not begin to match, or even understand. This had been said so often that by and large the Bagthorpes had come to believe it, and accorded him a grudging respect for it. And now here was Uncle Parker blithely talking about writing scripts for a hobby and relaxation, as if it were golf, or growing dahlias. Mr Bagthorpe's whole status was teetering.

'Only doing a series of three to start with,' said Uncle Parker modestly. 'Being filmed on location in Corsica. Thought I'd go along, actually. Rather fun. D'you know, Henry, I'm beginning to understand what you see in it.'

Mr Bagthorpe, who had never been on location anywhere further afield than Wigan, clenched and unclenched his hands and teeth.

'Couldn't make a career of it, mind you,' mused Uncle

Parker, as if talking to himself. 'I like something with a bit more of a challenge, myself. A bit of bite.'

Mr Bagthorpe looked as if he might be going to bite, if he could muster the strength, and even Jack, who liked Uncle Parker, felt he was taking things too far. He usually enjoyed the rows that took place between his father and his uncle, but this one was too one-sided to be comfortable. He put his own oar in.

'My English master says everybody's got one novel in them,' he contributed, 'and I expect it's the same with scripts. I don't suppose you could write any more even if you tried, Uncle Parker. I mean – no offence.'

'None taken,' replied Uncle Parker graciously. 'Certainly the whole process was almost too easy to be true. Perhaps I *have* shot my bolt.'

'Well, I think it's terribly exciting,' said Mrs Bagthorpe warmly, 'and so nice to have another String to your Bow. I often wish Henry would try to develop more Strings to his. It's such a mistake to become obsessively single-minded, I always think. Roundedness is the thing.'

She sounded as if she had slipped into being Stella Bright, and was certainly so far removed from present reality that she was failing to register her husband's problem. It was only after Mr Bagthorpe had lurched wordlessly from the room that she seemed to come to herself.

'Oh dear!' she exclaimed remorsefully. 'That was dreadfully tactless of me. Poor Henry!'

'If you ask me,' observed Mrs Fosdyke, whom no one *had* asked, 'a bit of competition never did anyone any 'arm. I should like to say congratulations, Mr Parker, and inquire when we might be seeing these plays, it not being August, I hope, when I shall be in the Isle of Man with my sister.'

'Thank you, Mrs Fosdyke,' replied Uncle Parker. 'And

certainly I shall let you know. Do you think I laid it on rather thick with Henry?' – this last to Mrs Bagthorpe.

'I do,' Jack said promptly. 'I think it was a bit thick, if you don't mind my saying.'

'He's had such a lot to put up with lately,' Mrs Bagthorpe said, 'and writing is such dreadfully exhausting and draining work. But of course, you know that,' she added, surveying the serene brow and relaxed pose of Uncle Parker, and mentally comparing them with her spouse's haggard mien.

'I was only trying to needle him,' Uncle Parker explained apologetically, 'just to get things going. I didn't know he'd take it quite so hard. Just thought we'd have a good slanging match. Been quite looking forward to telling him.'

There was a silence. The whole thing had certainly fallen flat, leaving Mr Bagthorpe devastated and everyone else feeling guilty.

Jack went up to tell the others, who were crowded around the airing cupboard on the second floor, gazing spellbound at a writhing mass of white maggots, as if witnessing a miracle.

'Crikey!' Rosie shuddered deliciously. 'Oooh, I can hardly

bear to look. You are clever, William. Real live maggots from real dead meat.'

Jack himself was equally impressed and, like Rosie, inclined to give William, rather than nature, credit for the mystery.

'Jolly good, William,' he said admiringly. 'I never thought it'd work.'

'When I do experiments, they work,' replied William.

He reached into the depths of the cupboard and retrieved bags and saucers of moulds and fungus, ranging from smooth to furry and from greyish white to green. The Bagthorpes, awestruck, regarded them. They were truly horrible.

'I give her two days,' observed William at length. 'At the outside.'

'She can't stand *flies*, even,' Jack said. 'Should we just have stuck to flies and things, d'you think?'

None of the others bothered to answer. Jack's unwillingness to go to extremes was one of the things that marked him out as irreversibly ordinary, that ruled out his ever being a genius. He was totally lacking in the necessary ruthlessness and obsessiveness that characterized his siblings. All of them would have been quite prepared to raise a boa constrictor in the airing cupboard to suit their purposes, had the thing been feasible.

If the family had had a motto, it would have been something along the lines of 'Enough is not Enough' or even 'Too Much is Never Enough'. Or, as Mr Bagthorpe had himself suggested, 'If a Thing's Worth Doing, It's Worth Overdoing.'

Only Jack was ordinary, and did things in an ordinary way. And he was in the minority, and in no position to stop a headlong Bagthorpian career once it had started, even if it was a career to disaster.

Chapter 5

The Dogcollar Brigade were due to arrive in the mid afternoon. Anyone else would have arrived in time for lunch, Mr Bagthorpe said, but Aunt Penelope would not allow Uncle Claud to drive at more than forty miles per hour even on motorways. Also, they intended to picnic on the way, and would naturally have to make a detour to do this, because Aunt Penelope would not want her family taking in exhaust fumes with their hermetically sealed sandwiches. A quick snack in one of the Motorway Stations was out of the question.

'I did suggest it,' Mrs Bagthorpe said, 'but you could almost see her going pale at the thought, even over the telephone. She really does have rather a complex about germs.'

'Was her maiden name, by any chance,' inquired her husband, 'Lister?'

The young Bagthorpes would normally have contrived to be well out of the way when the D.B. arrived, and to stay there as long as possible. On this occasion, however, they wanted to be present, partly because they were by now in a state of high excitement and anticipation over their maggots and moulds, and partly to reassure themselves that the Sainted Aunt had not undergone a personality change.

'It would be just our luck,' William said, 'if she'd been to a psychiatrist and got cured. Father did suggest it, you know, last time she came.'

'Even if she had, she'd be just as awful,' Jack said. 'There's all the texts and parables and things, remember.'

'Maggots and mould will not cure her of that,' William pointed out. 'Our whole strategy would be useless.'

'I wonder how you *do* cure people of texts,' Rosie said thoughtfully. 'Do you know what she said to me last time, when I showed her my self-portrait? She said "Vanity, vanity, all is vanity", and I think that was a really horrible thing to say, because I hadn't tried to make myself look pretty at all. Mother said it didn't even do me justice.'

After lunch, which was a sketchy affair because Mrs Fosdyke wanted to save herself for the evening meal, Grandma announced that she was going up to change.

'I have a strong sense of occasion,' she claimed, looking pointedly at Mr Bagthorpe's open-necked shirt and baggy jeans.

'You tell me when there's an occasion,' he replied, 'and I'll dress for it.'

'Perhaps you should tidy yourselves up a little, darlings?' Mrs Bagthorpe told her children hesitantly. 'Just as a gesture.'

'All right,' agreed William surprisingly, and flashed a warning look at the others, who all had their mouths open ready to protest.

'It's *strategy*,' he told his indignant siblings on their way upstairs. 'We must look as if we're being cooperative, to avert suspicion.'

Had he known it, Mrs Bagthorpe was already vaguely disturbed by so ready an agreement to her suggestion. For her children to leap to tidy themselves was much out of character.

'Though perhaps they are genuinely pleased that they are to see their cousins,' she told herself, because she tried to Think Positively whenever possible.

When the D.B. car rolled sedately up the drive of Unicorn

House at just after four, the younger Bagthorpes ranged themselves tidily and politely behind their mother on the steps to greet them.

Uncle Claud and his offspring were the first to get out. Aunt Penelope remained in her seat with her eyes closed. She always, she had told Mrs Bagthorpe, offered up a prayer of thanks for her family's safety after a journey, however short.

'For one may be killed on a short journey as easily as on a long one,' she said.

She sometimes missed connections on account of this practice. She sat in waiting-rooms with her eyes shut while her train drew out.

It was easy enough to greet Uncle Claud pleasantly because he was so inoffensive and had a nice smile. He seemed a genuinely happy man, which struck the Bagthorpes as astonishing, considering what he had to live with.

'How lovely to see you, Claud,' enthused Mrs Bagthorpe, embracing him. 'And Mother is so thrilled that you could come. And how are you?' she inquired of her nephew and niece, who were standing formally waiting to be noticed.

'Quite well, thank you, Aunt Laura,' they replied in unison.

'It's very nice of you to have us,' added Esther.

'We like coming here, because of the cooking,' said Luke, with patent truthfulness. He was a stout child, who evidently had regular access to food not supplied by his mother, and of a sweet and unwholesome variety, judging by the spottiness of his complexion. His eyes behind his spectacles were small and unwinking and missed nothing.

Rosie, being nearest in age to Esther, stepped forward, prompted by a nudge from Tess.

'Hallo,' she said. 'I'm building a house in a tree, and you'll be able to help.'

This was doubtful in the extreme. In the first place, Esther was unlikely to jeopardize the outstanding neatness of her person by monkeying about in a tree, and in the second, her mother would almost certainly forbid it. There were definitely insects in trees, and the one in question was particularly suspect.

'You try convincing *her* humans can't catch Dutch Elm disease,' William said.

Aunt Penelope herself now advanced, blinking a little. She was tall and white, with limp, useless-looking hands and she moved gropingly, like someone playing Blind Man's Buff.

Mrs Bagthorpe greeted her warmly but did not embrace her or even take her hand. Nobody ever embraced Aunt Penelope, and nor did she offer her hand. Nobody had seen her embrace her own children, even, and Mr Bagthorpe had once observed that the fact that Aunt Penelope had children at all was enough to make one consider seriously the proposition that they were found under gooseberry bushes.

She stood at a safe distance from the Bagthorpes and bestowed her blessings on them while they stared back at her unmoved. All of them forgot that they had meant to smile and look welcoming. She observed that they had grown, and they did not contradict her.

Grandma then appeared. She was got up in a way that would have been very flattering to most visitors, but even as she was embracing Claud you could see that Aunt Penelope was mentally saying 'Consider the lilies of the field...' Grandma looked not even remotely like a lily of the field, being elaborately coiffured, bedecked with rings and brooches and sporting a fair acreage of lace. She had probably gone to all this trouble to annoy Aunt Penelope, and to show Mr Bagthorpe that she considered her elder son worth such trouble.

'Now let's go and have a nice cup of tea!' cried Mrs Bagthorpe with an extremely hospitable air.

'Oh, but we must wash our hands first,' responded Aunt Penelope. 'Children, go upstairs and wash your hands thoroughly.'

Aunt Penelope was herself conducted to the downstairs lavatory, and seconds after she had bolted herself in, there was a scream. The younger Bagthorpes had been anticipating this, because they had accurately foreseen what her first move in the house would be, and had accordingly placed a spider in a strategic position on the hand-basin. Everyone else, however, was taken quite unawares, and stared apprehensively at the closed door. It was almost immediately thrown open.

'Oh!' shrieked Aunt Penelope. 'Oh, oh oh! Spiders!'

'Only *one*,' objected Rosie and promptly had her foot trodden on by Jack. He had been worried that the spider might get away before Aunt Penelope saw it, and had put two more in there for luck.

'There must be a *nest*!'

Aunt Penelope stood shuddering while Mrs Bagthorpe, exclaiming 'Surely not!', went to investigate.

'How very extraordinary,' she said, reappearing. 'They must have climbed up the waste pipe. Do go and move them, Jack.'

Jack willingly went and recaptured them, though they were very lively. He put them in the box he kept at all times in his pocket ready for the accommodation of insects. It seemed a pity to waste three good spiders that could easily be used again, though he was cunning enough to do a good deal of running of water, to convey the impression that the spiders were being drowned.

The party eventually assembled in the kitchen for tea and cakes, because the dinner table had already been laid out in the sitting-room.

'I do apologize for this,' Mrs Bagthorpe said, 'but we simply haven't had time to redecorate the dining-room.'

Mrs Fosdyke was enchanted to be entertaining on her own home ground, and greeted everyone warmly. She was a notoriously bad judge of character, and thought the Reverends were lovely people. She in particular preferred the D.B. offspring to the young Bagthorpes, and did much clucking over them and pressing of cream cakes. Normally they would not have been allowed more than one each, but after her second cup of tea Aunt Penelope rose and said that she wished to go up to her room and rest.

As she left, the young D.B. exchanged looks because they had designs on the cakes, and the young Bagthorpes exchanged looks because they were confident that Aunt Penelope was in for anything but a rest. They waited expectantly, but heard nothing. As William later pointed out, no one could expect a one hundred per cent success rate in a war waged with live insects which had a tendency to wander. Tess had suggested that the insects distributed should perhaps be dead ones, but was overruled.

'If they're not creeping and crawling,' said Rosie with relish, 'they won't scare the pants off her the same. And think, one might even creep and crawl *on* her while she's not looking!'

It was generally agreed that this latter contingency would be the ultimate triumph, and the insects were reprieved.

Jack and Rosie, who had been elected to shadow Luke and Esther, did not have much to do in the interval between tea and supper, because the visitors were hanging around Mrs Fosdyke and her food.

'We're having melon for starters,' Jack heard her tell them, 'you know – tickled up with wine, and a few glassies on top.'

He tiptoed away, gleefully anticipating Aunt Penelope's reaction when she tasted the wine, and went back to his room. He wanted to have another thumb through the Bible, to see if he could find any more texts that stuck up for dogs. So far, he had only one, though it was quite a good one, he thought, and unbeatable as long as the Sainted Aunt did not counter with some text *against* dogs. By and large the Bible did not seem much in favour of dogs, and tended to lump them in with whoremongers and murderers, Jack found.

'But you'll be all right, old chap,' he told Zero. 'I'll stick up for you. And I daresay even Father will, actually.'

The moment when Mr Bagthorpe actually confronted the guests inexorably arrived. He had gone to the library in Aysham that afternoon to be out of the way, leaving his wife to apologize for his absence.

The party foregathered at around seven, drawn irresistibly by the delicious scents of Mrs Fosdyke's cooking. Because the sitting-room was already much cluttered with extra dining furniture, Mrs Bagthorpe had wanted to dispense pre-supper drinks from a tray in Mr Bagthorpe's study. He had reacted strongly against this suggestion.

'If I ever got her vibrations in there,' he had said (meaning Aunt Penelope's), 'I do not think I should ever get rid of them. They would render me, and the room, sterile.'

There were, however, several comfortable chairs, the overflow from the sitting-room, placed about the hall, and there Uncle Claud and Aunt Penelope were sitting, tomato juice in hand, when Mr Bagthorpe emerged from his study. (He later asked his wife if she could arrange for Aunt Penelope not to sit in the hall, as he was sure he could feel her vibrations coming under the door. Mrs Bagthorpe did not see how she could promise this, so he fetched an old rug which he intended to place along the bottom of the door as a vibration-cum-draught excluder.)

'Ah, Henry!' exclaimed Aunt Penelope. 'So *there* you are!'

She sounded faintly accusing, as if she suspected him of having been in hiding – as, of course, he had been.

'Hello, there,' replied Mr Bagthorpe. 'How are you both? Looking remarkably in the pink, the pair of you!'

This remark sounded harmless enough, but was deliberate provocation, because Aunt Penelope always maintained that she was in poor health. Her complaint was obscure, its symptoms were mysterious and sudden in their comings and goings, and it had no known medical name.

'I am, as a matter of fact, not at all well, thank you,' she replied now. 'Though I do not complain.'

'Good,' said Mr Bagthorpe cheerfully. 'I have been frail myself latterly, but I don't complain.'

He went over and poured himself a stiff whisky. Jack watched Aunt Penelope as his father did this, and was rewarded by seeing the expected dark flush creeping up her neck. When Aunt Penelope refrained from criticizing, or coming out with a reproving text, her neck invariably went red. Jack thought this phenomenon very interesting.

Preliminaries over, conversation languished.

'Last week, Claud and I unavoidably stayed overnight in a guest-house in Worthing,' Aunt Penelope remarked suddenly. 'Unfortunately, it was unclean.'

Aunt Penelope did not use the word 'dirty'. To her, if things were not clean, then they were unclean, as they would have been in the Old Testament.

'Unclean, eh?' rejoined Mr Bagthorpe. 'Sorry to hear that. Very bad luck. While I think – give my car a wash down first thing tomorrow, will you, Jack? That's unclean.'

He tossed off the rest of his drink and helped himself to another.

'I think we can all go in now,' said Mrs Bagthorpe swiftly, putting down her craven orange juice and rising.

They went into the sitting-room and sorted themselves out round the table. This was something of a power game.

No one present wished to sit next to Aunt Penelope. Rosie and Uncle Claud lost. Mr Bagthorpe set about the wine.

'Not for us, thank you, Henry,' said Aunt Penelope.

'Really? On the wagon? Oh, bad luck!' He affected not to remember that the D.B. were unremittingly teetotal. 'Ah, well. As St Paul says in his First Epistle, Verse 23 "Drink no longer water, but use a little wine for thy stomach's sake. . ." '

'Of course, if one takes anything out of context. . .' said Aunt Penelope, very tight-lipped and thrown off balance.

His own family stared at him dumbfounded. Had he made it up, they wondered? Mr Bagthorpe almost never quoted from the Bible, and even if he did, he got it all wrong, and it never *sounded* like something from the Bible. This quote had sounded authentic, and if it was real, then he had certainly worked at it. What they did not know was that Mr Bagthorpe's journey to the library that afternoon had been partly to gain access to Cruden's *Concordance*. He had spent over an hour in the Reading Room looking up headings like 'wine' and 'word' and so on. He had also later leafed through the Old Testament, and come up with some useful material, particularly from Ezekiel and Lamentations.

Before Aunt Penelope had time to cap this very reputable-sounding quote, Mrs Fosdyke hedgehogged in with her tickled-up melon. She whipped a dish in front of everyone, and darted out again.

'Lovely,' murmured Mrs Bagthorpe, and picked up her spoon.

'Ahem!' Aunt Penelope cleared her throat loudly. 'Have we not forgotten something?'

'What's that?' inquired Mr Bagthorpe through a mouthful of melon.

'Grace,' she told him. 'Grace, Claud!'

Claud obediently shut his eyes and started in on what seemed an interminable grace, and Rosie giggled because she had forgotten about the grace aspect of the D.B. visits. Jack squinted across and saw that Aunt Penelope had her eyes shut very tightly, as if as a reproach.

At last Jack was free to deal with his glacé cherries, and did so, moving them into the melon and its juice.

'Stop!' commanded Aunt Penelope, and everyone jumped, and stared at her over their poised spoons. 'Esther, Luke, put down your spoons!'

There was a little clatter as they obeyed.

'Sorry,' said Mr Bagthorpe. 'Was there a second verse?'

'This melon,' stated Aunt Penelope, 'has been *tampered* with. Claud – your spoon!'

Another clatter.

'Do you not *like* the melon?' asked Mrs Bagthorpe anxiously. She was evidently uncertain whether, as hostess, she should put down her own spoon in sympathy, though none of the rest of her family had any such scruples. Grandma had nearly finished her portion.

'Alcohol has been poured on this melon,' Aunt Penelope told her. 'None of us will touch it.'

'Oh, I *am* sorry!' cried Mrs Bagthorpe. 'Oh, how terrible! I simply don't – would you like me to fetch you some clean ones – I mean fresh?'

'Pray don't trouble, Laura,' Aunt Penelope told her. 'We shall wait for the next course.'

Both her children looked downcast, having only got as far as the suspect cherries.

When Mrs Fosdyke came to remove the dishes she was much put out.

'Oooh, whatever's the matter?' she wanted to know. 'Oooh, not gone off, have they?'

'Alcohol, Mrs Fosdyke,' Aunt Penelope told her. 'Do not let it trouble you. I expect that you had your instructions.'

'Pray remove the dishes, Mrs Fosdyke,' said Mr Bagthorpe, cheerfully dispensing wine for his own family, including William. 'Delicious, I thought myself.'

Mrs Fosdyke looked little comforted by this, as if she knew that it was not so much a compliment to herself as a glancing blow aimed at Aunt Penelope. She rattled all the dishes on to a tray, and departed in moderate dudgeon.

It was when Mrs Bagthorpe removed the lid of the casserole that the meal really started to collapse. As the savoury steam rose up, amid much appreciative sniffing and twitching of noses around the table, Aunt Penelope exclaimed:

'Meat!'

She sounded thoroughly aghast.

'Boeuf Bourguignonne,' nodded Mrs Bagthorpe happily. 'Mrs Fosdyke's speciality.'

Her brow clouded slightly as she remembered that the dish would have been flamed in brandy and simmered in red wine, but cleared as she reflected that Aunt Penelope would be unlikely to know this. As it happened, alcohol was not to be the issue at stake.

'Laura,' said Aunt Penelope, 'surely you were aware that we had all been converted?'

Mr Bagthorpe looked up hopefully at this. If they had all been converted to Buddhism or Transcendental Meditation, there would be less evoking of the Old Testament.

'Converted?' echoed Mrs Bagthorpe, ladling a generous portion of the stew and passing it to Tess. 'Pass this down to your Aunt, dear.'

The plate was handed down and set before Aunt Penelope, who turned away her head as though she thought even the smell would corrupt her.

'We have become vegetarians, Laura,' she said. 'Surely I told you? I have told everybody. And I can hardly believe that, having been converted ourselves, we should not have attempted to convert our own family. We have been spreading the Word everywhere we go.'

'I can imagine,' said Mr Bagthorpe. 'Pass that plate to your grandmother, William. It'll be getting cold. Carry on ladling, Laura. We can be eating while Penelope tells us about it.'

From then on the meal went rapidly downhill. The younger Bagthorpes heartlessly carried on eating while the storm raged about them. Mrs Fosdyke was summoned, and on being asked to supply bowls of lettuce, grated carrot and apple, began to show signs of handing in her notice.

'Never mind, Mrs F.,' Mr Bagthorpe told her. ' "Man is born unto trouble as the sparks fly upwards." Job 5, Verse 7. And "All is vanity and vexation of spirit." Ecclesiastes 1, Verse 14.'

He had hardly dared hope to get his texts in so early on. Aunt Penelope was not really listening because she was off on her own tack, talking about 'abhorring all manner of meat' and about flesh, and blood, and so forth. Her offspring looked so bleak that Jack actually found himself feeling sorry for them. Grandma, who seemed already to have forgotten that it was at her own express wish that the D.B. had been summoned, was interrupting Aunt Penelope between mouthfuls of stew. She eventually turned upon her elder son.

'*You* have some stew, Claud,' she told him. 'Where is your spirit? Has your blood turned to water?'

Before he had a chance to reply, Mrs Fosdyke reappeared

and slammed down two bowls of salad and one of apples.

'I hope these'll satisfy,' she said. 'I didn't use no mayonnaise, because I didn't know if it would suit.'

' "Cast not your pearls before swine," Mrs F.,' nodded Mr Bagthorpe, hugely delighted by the way things were going. 'Quite right! *Are* you allowed mayonnaise, Penelope?'

Ignoring him, she stretched out a hand, took an apple, and began to peel it.

'Correct me if I am wrong,' continued Mr Bagthorpe, 'but didn't all the trouble *start* with an apple . . . ?'

In the ensuing silence he reached out and poured himself some more wine.

Chapter 6

It seemed to Jack that the visit of the D.B. would be both brief and eventful even without the introduction of moulds and maggots. Already half the household were at odds with one another. The only really happy people were the young Bagthorpes themselves, Grandpa, who always managed to be happy because of not hearing most of what was going on, and Mr Bagthorpe himself. The latter was highly elated. He advised his wife to hold the Family Reunion the very next day, instead of waiting until towards the end of the week.

'By the end of the week,' he told her, 'Fozzy will have gone for good.'

It was certainly interesting to see how rapidly Mrs Fosdyke's opinion of the D.B. changed when she found her culinary triumphs rejected. To reject her food was evidently to reject Mrs Fosdyke. Mrs Bagthorpe had to hold a long, conciliatory conversation with her, and allow her to let off all her feelings. She described this conversation as 'therapy'.

'My late husband had a sister who went on to the vegetables,' Mrs Fosdyke said, 'and she went right down to nothing. Not a skerrick of flesh on her bones. She died in the end, of course, and the doctor said it was natural causes, but my hubby used to say she died of too many vitamings. "An overdose of lettuce Kitty died of" – that's what he used to say.'

'How dreadful!' murmured Mrs Bagthorpe, neglecting to point out the unlikelihood of this.

'*And* there was this man in my newspaper that died of carrot juice,' went on Mrs Fosdyke morbidly. 'Went bright yellow and died.'

'I don't think it at all likely that any of them will die while they are here,' Mrs Bagthorpe assured her, 'and you are so clever with salads.'

Grandma was very withering about the whole thing.

'I consider lettuce leaves and cucumber to be garnishes,' she said. 'You cannot bring up a family on garnishes. And if Claud had ox liver twice a day, he might have more fight in him.'

All in all the atmosphere was so fraught that the young Bagthorpes decided to hold off with the maggots and mould for the time being.

'After all,' Rosie observed with satisfaction, 'they'll be growing and growing all the time, and getting even horribler!'

Luke and Esther were even beginning to be viewed sympathetically by their cousins, when the blow fell.

At the time all six of them were sprawled on the steps of the terrace after breakfast, wondering how they were going to get through the day.

'We're all going swimming this morning,' Tess told their guests. 'You'll come too, won't you?'

This strategy had already been decided upon. They were well aware that Aunt Penelope never allowed her children to go to swimming baths, which were full of germs and chemicals.

'We can't,' Luke replied. 'Mother won't let us. And in any case, I have to do three hours' Testing and Assimilation in the mornings.'

'To do *what*?' asked Tess.

Esther said, 'Luke's going to be the Young Brain of Britain.'

This challenging claim put all the young Bagthorpes, with the exception of Jack, instantly on their mettle. It emerged that Luke had been selected out of thousands of applicants to take part in a radio Quiz to find the Young Brain of Britain. He had already gone into training for this, including the three-hour session each morning with the *Encyclopaedia Britannica.*

'I already know most of what's in there,' he told them, 'but Mother tests me to refresh my memory and help me assimilate it.'

'I don't believe it,' William said flatly.

They all looked at Luke's large, baby-shaped head and tried to imagine the contents of the *Encyclopaedia Britannica* swimming around in there. They all came to the same conclusion.

'You're joking,' said Jack, voicing it.

Esther said primly, 'Luke doesn't make jokes do you, Luke? He's too clever to make jokes.'

'Esther's clever as well,' Luke testified, 'but in a different way. She's being published.'

Things were rapidly becoming unbearable.

'What do you mean, published?' demanded Rosie, who, being nearest in age to Esther, felt most threatened.

'She's having poems published in a book,' Luke said. He and Esther did one another's boasting. 'There's a book being published of all the best poems in England by children. She's got more poems in than anyone. She's got four.'

'Let's hear one, then,' Rosie said. 'Go on, Esther, say one.'

Esther said, 'I'm shy.'

'Have any of you ever had anything published?' Luke asked.

'We haven't tried,' Tess told him loftily. 'It has never occurred to us to try. In this family, poetry is the province of Aunt Celia. And as none of us wish to emulate her, or risk eventually becoming like her, we have tended to leave poetry severely alone. Which is the largest member of the Monkey Family?'

This last question was addressed to Luke, who promptly replied:

'The Mandrillus Sphinx of Equatorial West Africa. And the smallest is the Pygmy Marmoset.'

This was evidently correct, because Tess tossed her head and said:

'I must go and finish the last chapter of Voltaire, then practise for my solo at the Town Hall next month.'

She left.

'I think we're all going swimming this afternoon, as well,' Jack then said, feeling rather cunning. It would be an alibi, anyway. Rosie and William cast him grateful looks.

'I couldn't go anywhere anyhow,' Luke informed them. 'I do Headlines and Current Affairs in the afternoons.'

Headlines, they soon discovered, consisted of Luke's studying the *Guardian* for half an hour, and then being thoroughly tested on its contents by Aunt Penelope. She did not approve of the *Guardian* and thought most of its headlines incomprehensible because she did not seem to know about puns.

'We take in *The Times*, of course,' she told the Bagthorpes. 'I prefer my truth unvarnished.'

At lunch, when Mrs Bagthorpe heard about Luke's and Esther's successes, she was unselfishly delighted.

'How clever they both are!' she exclaimed. 'Did you hear that, darlings?'

Her own brood stared morosely at their plates – which were at any rate, unlike their cousins, swimming in gravy.

Mr Bagthorpe inquired, 'Did you say he *was* Young Brain of Britain, Penelope, or that he was making an attempt at this title?'

'The latter,' she replied, 'though we think the outcome is a foregone conclusion.'

She had fallen straight into the trap he had set to spring another of his texts.

' "Pride goeth before destruction and a haughty spirit before a fall". Proverbs 16, Verse 18.'

Aunt Penelope chewed stonily at her carrot.

'Now, what about the party?' Mrs Bagthorpe said gaily. 'Shall we say tomorrow?'

This was decided upon. Mrs Fosdyke, however, was by now so disillusioned that it really did seem as if she might give notice. There were already signs of malingering. That morning she had said to Mrs Bagthorpe:

'I think I might have to have a day or two at the dentist. My teeth are feeling strange.'

'They hurt? All of them?'

'No, I can't say that.'

'Your gums are bleeding, perhaps?'

'There ain't no blood, and they don't hurt.'

'Then I don't quite ...?'

'They feel strange,' repeated Mrs Fosdyke obstinately. 'They don't feel right to me. I asked Mrs Pye only last night if she'd look in my mouth, but she wouldn't. Said that kind of thing made her come over all tizzicky.'

When Mrs Bagthorpe told the family about this conversation they all agreed that it was a bad sign. If Mrs Fosdyke's teeth were feeling strange, trouble was clearly brewing.

While Luke was doing his Headlines and Esther probably composing poetry, the young Bagthorpes held a meeting under the hedge at the far side of the meadow. They had their swimming gear with them, but had no intention of going to the pool again. They would merely dampen everything in the stream before returning home.

Rosie, still probably the most threatened among them, was in favour of bringing out the live insects, maggots and moulds in force.

'But then there wouldn't be a Reunion Party,' Jack reminded her, 'and Grandma would be disappointed.'

'Let's bring them out *at* the party, then,' Rosie said.

This was considered to be a sound suggestion. It would ensure not only that Grandma got her party, but also that it would be an outstandingly lively one.

'There'll be a real row,' Rosie said, 'and Grandma'll love that.'

The Bagthorpes, however, were not going to be satisfied with merely retaliatory action. For some time now – ever since the burglary – they had been feeling undermined. They had to do something to re-establish themselves in their own estimation, and also in that of the world, if possible.

'Young Brain of Britain!' said William ferociously.

'He'll be famous if he wins,' Rosie said. 'And that soppy Esther. The only one famous in this family is Father.'

'And Mother,' Tess said, 'even if nobody does know that she is Stella Bright.'

'Thank the Lord,' added William.

'And Zero,' Jack reminded them. 'He's famous.'

This served only to deepen the gloom.

'We could all be famous if we wanted to,' William told them. 'It's just a question of deciding on how.'

Their ideas began tamely enough, with Rosie, for instance, suggesting that a London art dealer should be called in to see her Portraits with a view to an Exhibition at the National Portrait Gallery, and Tess writing off to the Liverpool Philharmonic for an audition. William said that he would make a start with his drums on *Opportunity Knocks*. It was only later that their ambitions became overweeningly extravagant and they began to set their sights not merely on a transitory fame but on actual, indisputable immortality. For the Bagthorpes, only extremes were acceptable, even if they did take some time to work up to them. Like rolling stones they inexorably gathered momentum as they went. And they wasted no time gathering moss.

When they got back to the house they found that Mrs Fosdyke had gone home with her strange teeth, and that Aunt Penelope was in charge of the evening meal at her own insistence.

'It will be no trouble at all,' she said, 'and perhaps one of the children will go down to the village and obtain lettuce and carrots, which seem to be missing.'

Where a lot of the lettuce had gone was up to the top floor to feed the livestock in the jamjars. The maggots seemed to prefer meat.

Aunt Penelope, having once secured a foothold in the kitchen, became extremely bossy. She allowed people to have a light tea, with cakes, but objected to Zero's presence under Jack's chair.

Jack was ready with his first Biblical reference.

' "The dogs eat of the crumbs which fall from their masters' table",' he told her boldly. 'Matthew 15, Verse 27.'

She was only momentarily floored by this.

'In those days,' she said, 'people had, of course, no idea of hygiene. I often think it was a miracle that Our Lord survived. The existence of bacteria was unknown.'

'Well, anyway,' Jack said, ' "A living dog is better than a dead lion," – Ecclesiastes 9, Verse something-or-other.'

'A *what*?' she repeated, turning from the sink.

Jack knew it was going to sound even worse the second time.

' "A living dog is better than a dead lion." Ecclesiastes 9, Verse whatever it is.'

'I do not imagine,' she said coldly, 'that any of us would dispute that. Fortunately, dead lions are seldom found in kitchens. And I think I have made quite clear my own preference as regards the dog.'

'He always sits under Jack's chair,' William said. 'We're pretty sure he hasn't got fleas.'

Aunt Penelope squeaked at this and threw up her wet hands in a shower of spray.

'Thank goodness that dog isn't ours,' Luke said. He had always wanted a dog, but would never get one. 'We think it's really embarrassing, that advert he does. Not to mention those awful soap and toothpaste ones of Grandma's.'

'*And* that dreadful Happy Family programme you did at Christmas,' Esther said. 'Everyone at school kept asking me if those Bagthorpes were any relation.'

'Mother says you're giving Bagthorpe a bad name,' Luke contributed. She did not deny this, and he continued, 'But that *burglary* was the worst thing. I don't suppose I'll ever live that down at school.'

'If you're going to be Young Brain of Britain, I don't suppose anyone will want to speak to you anyway,' Rosie told him. 'I shall tell people you're no relation, if they ask me.'

'Thou shalt not lie,' Aunt Penelope told her.

'Did you say you wanted some lettuce fetching?' Jack asked. He did not often get good ideas, but he had one now. 'Come on, Rosie, we'll go.'

He kicked her ankle, and she said:

'Oooch! All right.'

'You had better buy six lettuces,' Aunt Penelope told them, 'and four pounds of carrots.'

In the end, William and Tess came too. Anything was better than the company of the D.B.

'She's played right into our hands,' Jack told them gleefully as they went down the garden. 'She's bound to wash the lettuce herself. And it'll be crammed with creepy crawlies!'

'Crikey! Yes!' William was impressed. 'I'll go back to the house, and fetch some down. Then I'll meet you here, and we'll spread them around in the lettuce.'

'Fetch plenty!' Rosie shouted after him. She skipped across the meadow swinging her basket and chanting happily, 'Maggots, mould and creepy crawlies! Maggots, mould and creepy crawlies!'

'Not mould,' Tess told her.

'But wriggly things. We can put one under every leaf!'

They all enjoyed doctoring the lettuce. They divided the maggots and insects and set about deploying them in a realistic way. Fortunately the lettuces were each encased in a plastic bag, so there was little chance of half the livestock escaping before they reached their intended target.

'If she only does a couple, and puts the others in the vegetable rack, they'll be all over the pantry by morning,' William observed with satisfaction.

Aunt Penelope's reaction to the lettuce left nothing to be desired. Her shrieks were loud enough to fetch Mrs Bagthorpe running, followed closely by Grandma. (Grandpa and Uncle Claud were out fishing all day, and Mr Bagthorpe stopped in his study. He said later that when he heard the shrieks he had assumed that Aunt Penelope was being murdered, and did not wish to risk interrupting this.)

When Grandma discovered the reason for the disturbance she was scathing. She pushed Aunt Penelope aside and swished her hands about in the sink, scattering lettuce leaves.

'Where is your spirit?' she demanded of her cowering daughter-in-law. 'You should be ashamed of yourself. Your absurd diet is turning your blood to water. What are you doing to my son?'

She gave the lettuce leaves several violent shakes and dropped them into the glass bowl. Jack noticed that several maggots were still in among them. He doubted whether Grandma had even seen them. She was not so much washing lettuce as playing a scene.

'There!' Grandma turned from the sink. 'People who eat lettuce must learn to live with the things that come out when they wash it. I suppose that scenes like this are an everyday occurrence for you. Have you considered what it must be doing to the nerves of your defenceless children?'

She gestured towards Luke and Esther, who had remained impassive throughout the performance. Luke, who had taken advantage of the diversion to cram a further two slabs of cake into his mouth, looked particularly solid and unaffected.

'They are shaking bags of nerves,' Grandma continued, with a fine disregard for accuracy. 'No wonder they are so pale and thin. I shall speak to Claud as soon as he returns. And do not trouble to quote a text at me, I shall not listen!'

She swept out, leaving Mrs Bagthorpe to pacify Aunt Penelope, who was all for leaving first thing the next day.

'She thinks she will be heard for her much speaking!' she cried, meaning Grandma. 'I do not believe she wanted a Family Reunion at all. I do not believe she knows the meaning of the words!'

Two hours later the whole party gathered round the dining-table in a highly charged hostile atmosphere. They gazed glumly at the bowls of salad and chopped nuts, and waited for grace.

'Amen, I suppose,' said Mr Bagthorpe at the end. 'Why are there no wine glasses? Who laid the table?'

'I prepared the meal, Henry,' Aunt Penelope told him, 'and my children laid the table. They have not been brought up to set out wine glasses.'

'Mine have,' he returned. 'Rosie, fetch the glasses. I'll get the bottle.'

He got up.

'Thou shalt not kill,' he reminded himself under his breath as he left the room. 'Exodus 20, Verse 13.'

Chapter 7

Mrs Fosdyke came in the following day to carry through the Family Reunion Party, but one had the impression that it might be for the last time. Her teeth feeling so strange was keeping her awake, she said, and she could hardly bring herself to get up in the mornings. It could be a nervous breakdown coming on, Mrs Pye had told her, it was one of the signs. Mrs Bagthorpe, alarmed, told her children that they were to assist Mrs Fosdyke in every possible way.

But if she had imagined that her strange teeth were going to make her the centre of attention, she was sadly mistaken. The whole day was destined to be action-packed, even by Bagthorpian standards, and started, literally, with a bang.

This bang was loud, and somewhere outside, and fetched most of the household out to investigate. By then there was also cursing (Uncle Parker), wailing (Aunt Celia), and delighted squeals (Daisy). Uncle Parker had had his first motoring accident. This had been widely predicted for years, and the only surprising thing, as Mr Bagthorpe could not resist pointing out, was that it had not been fatal. (The only fatality so far had been Thomas, the toothy ginger tom belonging to Grandma, who had been run over at almost exactly the point in the drive where the present crash had occurred.)

What had happened was that Uncle Claud, when he returned from his fishing trip the previous evening, had parked his car in front of the house just round the last bend in the drive, made blind by thick shrubbery. Uncle Parker had come racing up in his usual style, and rammed straight into the back of it. Directly in front of Uncle Claud's car, unfortunately, was Mr Bagthorpe's, and the impact had been such as seriously to involve that, too.

Mr Bagthorpe had difficulty in concealing his delight at what had happened.

'This must be the first multi-vehicle pile-up ever to occur in a private drive,' he asserted. 'I shall telephone the newspapers. What a story this will make! After all, you are a writer now, Russell, and any publicity is good publicity!'

(He did not, in fact, phone the papers, because he was not on speaking terms with them after their coverage of the Bagthorpe Burglary.)

The party soon sorted itself into two groups, one of which (principally the ladies), gathered in the kitchen sobbing and wailing, and the other of which spent a long time in the drive shouting and arguing and apportioning blame.

Uncle Claud's car had come off worst. It was quite telescoped. As Mr Bagthorpe pointed out, if Aunt Penelope had happened to be seated in it at the time, praying, she would have been killed. He thought this a fine irony, and repeated it several times.

Had Uncle Claud himself not been such a mild man, Uncle Parker would undoubtedly have accused him of dangerous parking on a blind bend, and not only disclaimed all responsibility, but gone after him for damages. As it was, Uncle Claud was so genuinely distressed by what had happened, and so apologetic, that the gravel was cut from under Uncle Parker's feet.

The entire party eventually entered the kitchen, where much confusion still reigned. Mr Bagthorpe did nothing to improve matters by dispensing liberal tots of brandy. He said that this was medicinal, for shock, but he looked more as if he were celebrating. The only ones who drank the brandy were himself, Uncle Parker, Grandma and Mrs Fosdyke, who said she would have just a drop, though she doubted if it would help.

After his third brandy Mr Bagthorpe was cheerfully telling Aunt Penelope:

' "Man is born unto trouble as the sparks fly upward!" Job 5, Verse 7.' He had suspected that he might be able to get this in quite a lot, and he seemed for the moment to have overlooked the fact that without a car the D.B. were not going to be able to leave the following morning, as they had planned. When he was later reminded of this by William, his mood underwent an abrupt change.

'Verily I say unto you,' he said, 'there is no silver lining but what it has a cloud, or whatever.'

Grandma had quite a lot of brandy, because she said the accident had brought back to her in all its awful detail the day Thomas had been killed. The trouble was, the more brandy she drank, the more she seemed to remember this.

'I can see him now,' she told them, 'that great, golden jewel of an animal, struck down in his glorious prime. A light went out of my life that day.'

'Poor Grandma Bag,' said Daisy sympathetically. 'Was there a lot of blood?'

'You should not speak so in front of the child!' Aunt Celia cried. 'So sensitive, and so impressionable!'

'I 'spect the blood was all over everywhere,' Daisy said speculatively.

The mention of blood seemed to rouse the Old Testament in Aunt Penelope, whom no one could stop describing what would have happened had her family been actually inside the car when Uncle Parker arrived. Mrs Bagthorpe kept on trying to tell her that the odds against a family going straight out after breakfast and sitting in their parked car were millions to one, but she could not be brought to see this.

'Dust to dust and ashes to ashes,' Mr Bagthorpe told her. 'That's the way it goes, Penelope, you know that.'

Grandma was irritated by Aunt Penelope's trying to steal the limelight with a purely hypothetical accident.

'No one is dead,' she told her sharply. '*I* am the only bereaved person here. I think I may have to go up to my room and lie down.'

Mr Bagthorpe agreed that this might be advisable in view of the quantity of brandy she had drunk so early in the day, and suggested that Aunt Penelope should do the same.

'My place is at my husband's side,' she replied frigidly. 'This is a time of trouble.'

'It's that, all right,' Mr Bagthorpe agreed. 'Eh, Russell? Going to shoot the Insurance up a bit, this lot, isn't it?'

Uncle Parker replied, 'There is one thing, Henry, a re-spray is not going to do your car any harm. Get some of your old dints and scratches thrown in at the same time. It's an ill wind.'

At this stage no one was bothering much about Uncle Claud's written-off vehicle, and he himself did not seem to like to bring it up.

Mrs Bagthorpe tried to create a more cordial atmosphere by exclaiming:

'You must stay to lunch, of course, now that you are here, Celia. Then we can have a Reunion Lunch *and* Party!'

Mr Bagthorpe pointed out that the Reunion was being organized solely for the benefit of Grandma, and that she would most probably still be sleeping at lunch-time. Mrs Fosdyke said that she had not counted on catering for lunch as well as tea, and Aunt Celia said that she wished to return to her own home as soon as possible.

'I have lost my sense of Cosmic Security,' she told them. 'I must try to recapture it before it is gone for ever.'

All this being so, Uncle Parker volunteered to organize the towing away of the three vehicles, and said he would ask the garage at the same time to send an extra car for his own use. Jack heard him ordering it over the telephone.

'And make it something *fast*,' he heard him say. 'It's these crawling jobs that cause all the accidents.'

'Can I stay?' Daisy asked. 'I want to stay and be with Grandma Bag because of poor Thomas.'

Aunt Celia was at first dubious about this, because she said that Daisy had had sufficient trauma for one day. But Rosie eagerly volunteered to keep an eye on Grandma, and make sure she did not say anything unsuitable.

'I've got lots of lovely things I can show Daisy,' she told Aunt Celia – meaning the maggots and moulds. Rosie was devoted to Daisy, mainly because she was younger, and had hardly any Strings to her Bow, if Aunt Celia's claims were discounted. With Esther around, Rosie needed Daisy more than usual. Aunt Celia reluctantly agreed.

'If Daisy asks for paper and pencil, give them to her immediately,' she told everyone. 'If she can write a poem about what has taken place, it will be cathartic. When I get home, I shall try to write one myself.'

Mr Bagthorpe endorsed this instruction.

'If she asks for paper and pencil and you don't supply it,' he warned, 'there is little doubt that she will begin writing her thoughts on the walls again.'*

In the event, Daisy showed no recognizable signs of wanting to write poems either on paper or on the walls. Later, most people present were to wish she had occupied herself half so harmlessly.

When the Parkers had gone Mr Bagthorpe returned to his study in high good humour, saying that he was in exactly the right mood for getting on with his script. His enjoyment of the morning had been heightened by the arrival of the breakdown men. They had been full of pithy humour about pile-ups in private drives, and had driven off laughing. By evening, it was certain, the entire neighbourhood would be in possession of the story, and the accounts given would doubtless be more highly coloured than any newspaper reports. As Mr Bagthorpe went into his study he was heard to say something about 'A Daniel come to Judgement' – probably, in his euphoric state, imagining this to be a Biblical reference.

Aunt Penelope and Luke retired to do their Testing and Assimilation, accompanied by Esther. The young Bagthorpes retreated to William's H.Q. to decide on their course of action. Daisy was allowed along too, though under sufferance.

'You *know* what she's like,' Jack told Rosie. When Daisy had done creative things with water, he himself had come in for a good share of the shouting.

* See *Absolute Zero*.

'She's sweet,' Rosie maintained, 'and she's only little. If she doesn't come, I'm not.'

Daisy was enchanted by everything in the airing cupboard, and particularly the maggots, which seemed to mean more to her than the moulds and fungi. This was probably because they were moving. She was allowed to take the saucers of maggots out and play with them while the others had their meeting.

'We can speak freely before her,' Tess told them. 'She will have not the slightest comprehension of what is transpiring.'

The main question was whether or not to carry through the doctoring of the Family Reunion tea. Jack was against this.

'It's a bit different now,' he argued. 'There's been a catastrophe. I don't think even the Sainted Aunt deserves *two* catastrophes in one day.'

The others were concerned not so much with whether she deserved them (which they were unanimous in believing she did) as whether she could stand up to them.

'If she gets hysterical,' William pointed out, 'or has a nervous breakdown, she might have to stop here for ages.'

'No, she won't,' Rosie said. 'People with nervous breakdowns have to have peace and quiet. I heard Fozzy say so. And she said there was no peace in this house.'

This was unarguable.

'So we go ahead?'

It was agreed that they should, with caution. Only half the maggots would be brought into play, and a fraction of the available mould and fungi. Jack was still unenthusiastic.

'We'll get into awful trouble,' he said.

'Only from Mother,' William said. 'Father'll probably slip us a fiver.'

'What about Fozzy? What if *she* goes and has a nervous breakdown?'

'In that case,' replied William heartlessly, 'he'll probably slip us a tenner.'

'What are they for?' asked Daisy, delightedly watching the rise and fall of maggots.

'They're a lovely surprise, for Aunt Penelope,' Tess told her. 'They're a treat. But we want to keep it an absolute secret, till the party. Can you keep a secret?'

'I promise,' said Daisy solemnly. 'What a lovely treat. Aunt Panoply is lucky.'

Lunch was a makeshift and rather silent meal. Grandpa and Uncle Claud had gone somewhere on a bus, and Grandma was still sleeping off her brandy. Aunt Penelope was being very tight-lipped, which Jack thought curious, considering how often she talked about forgiving people's trespasses. (Though he recognized that Uncle Parker's trespassing had been of an unusually radical nature.)

In the background Mrs Fosdyke was darting and muttering non-stop, and making a great issue of keeping separate the vegetarian dishes from those to be consumed by ordinary mortals.

'I should like to know why pigs was invented,' she was heard to say, as she garnished her beautifully raised pork pies, 'if not to be ate. Great ugly dirty things, and all the feeding they take. Pigs wasn't invented just to look at, that I do know.'

Jack himself thought the logic of this irrefutable, and wished that Mrs Fosdyke would put it directly to Aunt Penelope.

Daisy was unusually silent, and if the Bagthorpes had not been so caught up in their own conspiracies they might have noticed this, and been on their guard. If Daisy was quiet, it was probably because she was thinking, and when Daisy did any prolonged thinking it usually boded ill. Half-way through the meal she pushed her plate away and said:

'I've finished now, Auntie Bag. Please may I get down?'

'But there are stewed prunes to come, Daisy,' Mrs Bagthorpe protested.

'No, sank you, Auntie Bag,' replied Daisy politely. 'No prunes.'

'Very well, Daisy, you may get down,' Mrs Bagthorpe told her, knowing well that Aunt Celia insisted on Daisy's being given a free rein in all things, to encourage her creativity.

Daisy accordingly got down and trotted towards the door.

'Where're you going?' Rosie asked. 'I'll come in a minute, when I've finished.'

'I'm going to sit with Grandma Bag,' replied Daisy. 'I love Grandma Bag.'

Of this they were only too well aware. A powerful and uncanny empathy existed between the pair of them. In league they were so formidable as to have become known in the family, and with every reason, as the Unholy Alliance.

After lunch the young Bagthorpes were delegated to set out the table in the sitting-room, under their mother's supervision. Aunt Penelope said that she and her children would retire to their rooms and do Headlines and Current Affairs as usual. She did not, naturally, approve of parties, and wanted her offspring to be as little contaminated by the festivities as possible.

The table laid, the young Bagthorpes retreated to the upper storey to organize their saucers. Once up there William produced what he declared to be their trump card.

'If all else fails,' he told them, 'this will drive them from our doors for ever.'

He brought out a stoppered glass phial.

'Rotten eggs,' he told them. 'Worse. Who wants a sniff?'

They all did, they said, but were not prepared for the intensity of the stench that issued from the innocuous-looking yellow liquid.

'Put it back on, quick,' Jack gasped, meaning the stopper, and Rosie pinched her nostrils and rushed from the room.

'It's not poisonous, idiot!' William cried. 'Come back in.'

'Not till you've opened the window,' came the reply. 'Open it wide. Oooh, I feel sick!'

They all did.

'We're not using that,' Tess told William. 'Nobody'll be able to eat anything, if you let that stink out.'

'And Fozzy's done some really good stuff,' Jack said.

William, who must have had more resistance to the smell than the others, was much put out by the disappointing reception of what he considered to be his master-stroke.

'You lot,' he told them, 'are getting flabby. What's the matter with you? Come back in, Rosie!'

She reappeared, gingerly, still holding her nose. William dived into the airing cupboard and re-emerged with the plates and saucers, which he placed before them.

'Funny,' he said. 'There's hardly any maggots left.'

They all looked.

'They must've got loose,' Jack said. 'They must be all over the airing cupboard.'

A quick search failed to reveal more than a rather slow-footed spider, which was promptly bagged by Jack for his collection.

'They're jolly big,' Rosie said, eyeing the remaining maggots. 'What if they've eaten one another?'

No one present knew whether or not this was a possibility.

'There's one thing,' said William decisively, 'if that's all the maggots we've got, we're definitely using the smell.'

An altercation immediately set up. In the end, a compromise was decided upon. Fate should be allowed to determine the matter. The phial was to be balanced, lightly stoppered, concealed in the floral arrangement in the centre of the table.

'If there's any yanking or shoving,' William said, 'it'll drop, and either break or the top come off.'

His suspicious siblings immediately saw the flaw in this arrangement.

'You could *deliberately* do yanking and shoving,' Rosie told him. 'You've got to promise not to.'

'Swear not to,' said Jack, taking a leaf out of Grandma's book.

A swearing ceremony duly took place.

'Though I still think you're turning yellow,' William told them. 'The sooner we drive the Sainted Aunt out of here the better. I want to get down to being famous before any of the D.B. do.'

They all did, with the exception of Jack, and confidently awaited the outcome of the Family Reunion Party.

'Once that is over,' William maintained, 'it's unlikely this family will ever be united again.'

In this he was to be proved not only right, but right beyond anything he had expected or hoped for. Not only were branches to be rudely snapped from the Bagthorpe family tree, but it was about to be riven, as if by lightning, clear through.

Chapter 8

The Family Reunion was scheduled for six o'clock. Everyone, Mrs Bagthorpe had said, was to dress.

'This is a once in a lifetime occasion,' she told her family.

'And Amen to that,' said her husband. 'Hallelujah. I had better go and order a hire car for the Latter Day Saints, in the morning. I have premonitions of disaster.'

His offspring looked keenly at him. Could he have been up in the airing cupboard? He went into the hall and they heard him ordering the car.

'And make it something *slow*,' they heard him tell the garage, 'or they won't get into it.'

'They're bringing it over at four,' he told them. 'That'll give Penelope time to bless it, or consecrate it, or whatever.'

As the afternoon wore on the atmosphere became electric. Mrs Fosdyke was in her customary state of pre-party nerves, and hedgehogging about with doilies and covered trays. The young Bagthorpes were in a like frenzy of activity, made the more fraught by their having to dovetail their visits to the dining-table with those of Mrs Fosdyke. She was no easy person to dovetail with, even at the best of times, and today she seemed to possess to a more than usually marked degree the ability to be in three places at once. On one occasion William had to stand for quite a long time pretending to straighten the floral arrangements, because if he took his hand away quickly Fate might be forestalled, the phial spilled, and the game up before it had properly begun.

'You should let your Ma's flower arrangements alone,' Mrs

Fosdyke told him. 'Great strapping lad like you, fiddling about with flowers!'

This had made William feel extremely silly. Under normal circumstances he would not have been caught dead looking at a flower arrangement, let alone touching it.

'It was off balance,' he said defensively. 'I have a highly mathematical and logical cast of mind, and require exact proportion and symmetry in all things.'

'Rubbish!' Mrs Fosdyke told him, and was off again, giving William the opportunity to complete the exercise. He made certain the phial was precariously balanced.

'Good luck, Fate!' he said out loud, and retreated.

By mid-afternoon there was a temporary lull in activity. Rosie was in her room preparing her camera and flash equipment. She had decided against a portrait because she found the D.B. more or less unpaintable. Also, she thought there would be plenty of action at the party, and that it would best be captured by a high speed shutter. Jack was in his room, too. He was giving Zero a patting and praising session preparatory to breaking to him the news that he was not to attend the Family Reunion.

'It's nothing to do with the Sainted Aunt,' he assured him. 'I'd stick up for you against her till Kingdom come. It's this smell, you see, old chap. It's awful, it's really terrible. And you've got such a strong sense of smell, you've got a really great nose – just like a bloodhound. But it might get damaged, with being so sensitive. Good old boy. You've got the best sense of smell of anyone in this house. Good *boy*.'

Zero did not particularly prick up his ears at any of this.

'I'll save you some bits,' Jack promised him. 'Some of Fozzy's pork pie, and some garlic sausage.'

Zero's ears did prick up a little.

'You try and sleep through it,' Jack advised him. 'I wish I could.'

Daisy and Grandma were holed up together in Grandma's room – or so everyone assumed, until Grandma emerged looking for a cup of tea. She was in a very bad temper.

'*There* you are, dear!' Mrs Bagthorpe greeted her warmly. 'Did you have a nice sleep?'

'I haven't been asleep,' Grandma snapped. 'I have been thinking.'

The way she said this last word made Jack wonder whether she had taken up Thinking instead of Breathing* – which she had given up several months previously.

'Are those other wishy-washy relations of mine still here?' Grandma continued, having apparently forgotten the Family Reunion.

'Of course, dear,' Mrs Bagthorpe assured her. 'We're having the *party* today, remember. And wait until you see your cake! It's all –'

'There is no need to talk to me as if I were four years old, Laura,' Grandma interrupted coldly. 'Where is Daisy?'

'I – we – I thought she was with you,' said Mrs Bagthorpe lamely. 'Hasn't she been?'

'Laura,' said Grandma, 'if Daisy had been with me, would I be inquiring as to her whereabouts?'

'Of course not. But –'

'If that Daisy's loose,' put in Mrs Fosdyke at this juncture, 'I should like to see the sitting-room door locked. Begging your pardon, Mrs Bagthorpe. There's a lot gone into that meal, and I don't want it set fire to or flooded.'

'Of course not, Mrs Fosdyke,' Mrs Bagthorpe said.

Mrs Fosdyke was referring to proclivities of Daisy's now dormant – or as far as anyone knew. On the other hand, Mrs

* See *Ordinary Jack*.

Bagthorpe had the profoundest respect for Daisy's destructive creativity, and could not help feeling a slight uneasiness.

'Where can she be?' she wondered.

'You should keep her under your wing,' Grandma told her crossly. 'Have you no sense of responsibility? Daisy is only five years old – a shining jewel of a child. What if she has become trapped in the deep freeze?'

She only mentioned this possibility because she had recently read a case of the kind in her newspaper, but she said it as if she had some kind of inside information. Mrs Bagthorpe let out a faint moan and leapt to investigate.

'Oh, thank goodness!' she gasped, returning from the outhouse.

'She is not then dead, I take it?' Grandma said.

'Oh, don't say such things, Mother!'

Mrs Bagthorpe was spiralling into a state of considerable agitation, exactly as Grandma had intended she should. No one knew better than Grandma that Daisy was perfectly capable of looking after herself, and that wherever she went it was not she who came to grief, but other people.

'Would Mrs Bagthorpe Senior like to 'ave a look at 'er cake, Mrs Bagthorpe?' asked Mrs Fosdyke, as if Grandma were either deaf, or not present.

'Certainly not!' Grandma snapped, forestalling her daughter-in-law's reply. 'I want a surprise. When you get to my age, you don't get many surprises.'

'All right,' returned Mrs Fosdyke, faintly huffy. 'Though there's no surprises about *my* cakes, I should hope.'

'I hope there are going to be *some* surprises at my party,' Grandma said petulantly. 'I would like another cup of tea. Where is Daisy?'

Jack was dispatched to look for her, with some urgency on his mother's part.

'And don't tell your father,' she added. If Mr Bagthorpe knew that Daisy was at large, he would become unsettled and bitter.

Jack found Daisy quite quickly. She was sitting on the top stair looking perfectly composed, as if she had been there all afternoon, like a statue, while people walked round her.

'Hello, Daisy,' Jack said. 'Where've you been?'

'I been busy,' she told him.

This sounded ominous. In Jack's experience, no one knew how to be busy quite how Daisy knew how to be busy.

'What have you been doing?' he asked.

She shook her head.

'It's a secret,' she replied. 'It's a lovely secret for Grandma Bag.'

Jack was relieved. Daisy was undoubtedly fond of Grandma, insofar as she was fond of anybody. She was unlikely to have been destructive at Grandma's expense.

Jack still had a good deal to learn about the five-year-old mind in general, and Daisy's in particular. Definitions of what is destructive are at best hazy at this age, and in Daisy's case, the line between right and wrong was so blurred as to be virtually non-existent. She also had confused notions as to what kind of things made people happy.

'I don't like Auntie Panoply,' Daisy now confided loudly and inconsequentially.

'Ssshhh!' Jack told her. 'None of us do. She's going soon.'

'Good,' said Daisy. 'Where's Grandma Bag?'

'Looking for you,' Jack said. 'In the kitchen.'

The Unholy Alliance, reunited, decided to retire to Grandma's room to bedeck themselves for the party.

'Mummy's bringing my Pobble frock that hides my toes,' Daisy told everyone.

'Lovely, dear,' said Mrs Bagthorpe encouragingly. 'That *will* look nice.'

'Yes,' Daisy agreed complacently, 'I sink it will. It's going to be a very poetic party, 'cos I've got a surprise for Grandma Bag.'

At this Mrs Bagthorpe looked alarmed and Mrs Fosdyke scooted smartly from the room and turned the key in the sitting-room lock.

Aunt Penelope, Luke and Esther appeared.

'Just a cup of weak tea,' the former requested.

'I suppose you have spent the afternoon stuffing those children's brains with unnecessary information,' Grandma said, playing picador. 'They should have been in the open air, exercising their lungs and shouting. Why is it that those children never shout? It is quite unnatural.'

'We do not believe in raised voices at our house,' replied Aunt Penelope.

'Great heavens above!' Grandma was disgusted.

'Do go and look at the lovely car the garage have brought for you,' Mrs Bagthorpe swiftly interposed.

'It looks smashing,' Jack said. 'Better than your old one. It's red.'

'Red!'

Aunt Penelope went straight off to look, the rest followed, and they came out of the front door just in time to see Uncle Parker's second accident.

This was a carbon copy of the earlier one, except that the bang was not so loud, and Uncle Parker had a little longer to brake. Several people screamed.

'The Lord have mercy on us!' cried Aunt Penelope predictably.

'I'm off to fetch my camera,' said Rosie, and went.

'What is all this disagreeable commotion?' came Grandma's voice from within.

As it turned out, little damage had been done on this occasion, except to people's already jangled nerves. Aunt Celia, if she had succeeded in recapturing her sense of Cosmic Security, had clearly lost it again. She ran to Daisy and clasped her, crying irrationally:

'Oh, my darling! Thank heavens you are safe!'

Daisy disengaged herself so as to inspect the state of the vehicles.

'It's not very bad,' she said disappointedly. 'There's only some dents and things and some red glass broken.'

Uncle Parker tried to pass the incident over completely.

'Just a bumper to bumper job,' he asserted. 'What bumpers are for, of course. What imbecile put that car there? Does no one in this house learn from his mistakes?'

Unluckily Mr Bagthorpe emerged at this point, and took in the scene at a glance.

'Well, well!' he said. 'You know what they say. "As a dog returneth to his vomit so a fool returneth to his folly." Proverbs of course, Penelope, Chapter 26, Verse 11. You are well on your way to a hat trick, Russell.'

'There'll be a third,' came Mrs Fosdyke's voice in flat tones. 'Things always go in threes.'

'I will not be driven in that dangerous car,' said Aunt Penelope with finality.

Mrs Bagthorpe tried to point out to her that it was not her car that was dangerous, but Uncle Parker's. This she would not allow. She declared that their own hired car would now be irremediably bent and sprained underneath where no one could see it. Uncle Claud tried to reason with her, too, but ended up by himself ringing the garage and requesting that another car should be delivered.

'Something nice and steady, if you would be so good,' he said, 'and of a sober colour.'

The Family Reunion was by now off to a thoroughly bad start. In some families, the misfortunes of the day might have been taken as a sign that things were now bound to take a turn for the better. But with the Bagthorpes, when things were bad they inexorably went to worse, and this occasion was to be no exception.

At a quarter to six Mrs Bagthorpe made a desperate bid to salvage the situation by opening champagne. Several of the party, admittedly, perked up at this – notably Grandma, and Mr Bagthorpe – but others were evidently further alienated by it.

'It is a mystery to me,' Aunt Penelope said frostily, 'why some people cannot make merry without the aid of alcohol.'

'Not alcohol, Penelope,' Mr Bagthorpe corrected her. 'Bubbly. Try some. Do you good.'

Jack himself thought Aunt Penelope's remark uncalled for in that he himself had never seen her come anywhere near making merry with or without artificial aids.

Mrs Fosdyke was brought in to partake of the festivities. She had on her new best dress of turquoise crimplene, and held her glass with her little finger delicately raised. Mr Bagthorpe appointed himself toastmaster, and thought of so many things to toast that a second bottle had to be opened.

Grandma, who had not been toasted for years, mellowed visibly.

'Forty-four years a mother!' Mr Bagthorpe raised his glass. 'And here's to the next forty-four!'

Grandma, of course, was not supposed to drink to herself, but she did. She even chipped in with a toast of her own.

'And Alfred!' she said. 'He is forty-four years a father, remember. I should like to toast Alfred!'

She nudged Grandpa, who beamed and obediently raised his own glass as everyone drank to *his* next forty-four years.

'I think perhaps we might drink to Mrs Fosdyke's health,' said Mrs Bagthorpe, just as people were beginning to run out of toasts. 'She has not been feeling at all well of late, and has risen splendidly to the occasion.'

Glasses were recharged, and everyone drank to Mrs Fosdyke, including herself, who, having seen Grandma do the same, evidently thought it the done thing.

By the time the party repaired to the sitting-room at least half of them were in high spirits, and it almost seemed as if the occasion might be going to be a success after all. Even Mrs Fosdyke had become skittish, and darted about the table with unusual panache, whisking covers from dishes with the air of a conjuror producing rabbits from hats.

'Eat up!' she urged. 'Eat, drink and be merry!'

Jack himself felt not so much merry as apprehensive. He regretted the mould and maggots. It seemed to him that he and his siblings were gilding the gingerbread. The D.B. were to leave the following day in any case, so it was not even as if the maggots and mould were to serve any useful purpose.

As it turned out, Grandma's party was spoiled sooner than anyone could have anticipated. The company had barely settled themselves, grace had not yet been said, when Uncle Parker exclaimed:

'By Jove! Nearly forgot. Offerings, and all that. My felicitations, Mother. A little something in token of my appreciation for producing my beautiful wife.'

He rose, planted a kiss on Grandma's head, and placed a large packet before her.

'Oh dear,' Mrs Bagthorpe murmured, 'I never thought of a present.'

Grandma was patently pleased by this gesture, even coming from the assassin of Thomas.

'How very kind of you,' she told Uncle Parker, and began at once to pull at the wrappings.

'Good lord!' exclaimed Mr Bagthorpe as the final tissues were pulled aside. 'It's a resurrection!'

'Oooh! It's the spitting likeness!' screeched Mrs Fosdyke.

What Uncle Parker had given Grandma was a life-sized replica of the late Thomas. It was as if, Mr Bagthorpe later observed, someone had taken a death mask.

The appearance of this *objet d'art* reduced the table to a stunned silence. The size, gingeriness and malevolent aspect of the pottery cat were such that no one had ever seen the like. It was not the sort of thing anyone would ever want on a mantelpiece, and could hardly even be properly described as an ornament, any more than its original could have been.

'It is quite beautiful,' said Grandma at length.

She had not taken her eyes from the replica. She turned it about on the table before her, as if checking all the well-loved and remembered details – the length of the unsheathed claws, the sinister slant of the eyes, the bared teeth.

'Borrowed some of your photographs,' Uncle Parker told her, much pleased by the reception of his offering. 'Got one of Celia's arty chaps to do it. Like it, do you?'

There could be no doubt at all about this. Grandma was clearly casting about in her mind for a suitable niche where the pot Thomas could be enshrined. Daisy, evidently made jealous, got down from her seat and trotted round to the head of the table.

'*I've* got a present,' she announced. 'You'll like it, Grandma Bag. It's a lovely secret surprise.'

Grandma, made ecstatic by the champagne and her pot cat, embraced Daisy effusively.

'You darling child!' she cried. 'How blessed I am in my family!'

She had never said anything like this before, and everyone present could not but feel pleased. The box Daisy placed before Grandma was extremely lavishly wrapped, and doubtless accounted for Daisy's long absence during the afternoon.

'You're supposed to keep it a right way up,' Daisy told Grandma. 'But I've forgot which it is. Jus' open it. It's lovely.'

'That looks like the sash of my new long frock,' Tess exclaimed, referring to the mummy-like lengths of orange silk wrapped about the offering. It in fact was, cut into suitably narrow ribbons by the meticulous Daisy.

'It's not all for you, Grandma Bag,' Daisy told her, hopping from one foot to the other. 'Only the things *inside* the thing is yours, 'cos the other's Auntie Bag's that I borrowed.'

The meaning of this obscure utterance was soon to become clear. What immediately happened, however, was far from clear, and, as so often with Bagthorpian holocausts, no one was ever afterwards able to remember the exact sequence of events. They happened too quickly for anyone to be able to remember, and certainly for Rosie's high speed shutter to cope with.

The last layer of wrapping fell away, there was an ear-piercing scream from Grandma, and she threw up her hands, fetching the pot cat a cuff that sent it crashing to the floor. William, who was seated next to her, made a grab at it, and in so doing caught the tablecloth, and the cut-glass dish of Mrs Bagthorpe's that appeared to be Daisy's gift to Grandma flew up, in a shower of large white maggots.

Then everyone was either screaming or yanking at the tablecloth or scrambling to get clear. The Bagthorpes had a long history of making a clean sweep of party tables, and nearly everything ended up on the floor.

Grandma did not seem to be able to stop screaming, and was probably having hysterics, but nobody quite dared slap her on the face. Aunt Penelope and Aunt Celia screamed a lot as well, in horrible unison, and Daisy began to howl, and got down and tried to retrieve some of the scattered maggots. Jack ran to the top of the table to see if the pottery cat could be salvaged, but it was quite past repair.

'Never mind, Grandma!' he shouted above the din. 'Uncle Parker'll get you another.'

'Oooh! Oooooh!' Aunt Penelope's screams now hit a new, unbelievably high pitch. 'Poison! Oooooh! Quickly!'

The flower arrangement had gone over along with everything else, and the phial had become unstoppered. The stench seemed to hit everyone at more or less the same moment, and the doorway instantly became jammed with people trying to get out. Jack nobly hung back and, with his nostrils pinched, fumbled around with his free hand in the debris, to see if he could locate the phial and re-stopper it. In the end he ran out of air and had to retreat. He was the last out, and he slammed the door behind him and leaned against it, gasping for air.

Even in the hall the smell was seeping through. Mrs Bagthorpe ran to the front door and opened it wide.

'Outside!' she cried. 'Everyone outside and breathe deeply!'

Most people intended to do this anyway. The awfulness of the stench, and its total unexpectedness, were such that everyone was quite dazed by it. So powerful was it that later the sitting-room was to be fumigated, and all curtains and loose covers sent to the dry cleaners. Even after this people sometimes used to maintain that they could still smell it.

None of the younger Bagthorpes had ever imagined that Grandma's party would be as quickly and thoroughly disrupted as this. They fell silent, awed by the horrifying extent of their success. Jack saw, through the open door, a small figure scuttling away down the drive. Mrs Fosdyke had gone home.

Chapter 9

The Dogcollar Brigade wanted to leave immediately. Nothing, Aunt Penelope declared, would induce her to spend another night in the house with maggots roaming free and poisonous fumes penetrating everywhere. She telephoned some of her own relatives living forty miles away, and tried to arrange for her family to spend the night there en route for home.

It was clear from the Bagthorpe end of the conversation that she was making no headway. When she put down the telephone she said:

'Ruth and Samuel would dearly have loved to accommodate us, but suspect that they have scarlet fever in the house.'

'A likely story,' observed Mr Bagthorpe. 'I would never attempt to make a plot depend on such a contingency. Have they no imagination?'

'We shall have to stay!' said Aunt Penelope desperately. 'Come, children, come, Claud, put on your coats. We must stay outside as late as possible, breathing in pure air.'

'There is no use my pointing out, I suppose,' said Mr Bagthorpe, 'that to the pure all things are pure?'

'At least come into the kitchen first,' pleaded Mrs Bagthorpe, desolated by her titanic failure as hostess and convenor of Family Reunions. 'You have had nothing to eat.'

This cued Aunt Penelope in nicely.

'Man does not live by bread alone,' she said.

'I should rather like a little cake, dear,' said Uncle Claud timorously.

'So would we,' chimed in Luke and Esther promptly.

'We will have the cake,' said Mr Bagthorpe, 'and then we shall conduct the most bloody and thorough-going post mortem this household has ever known.'

His offspring blanched. This, in a family that specialized in post mortems, was a considerable prospect. They did not, of course, know that the statement was made principally for the benefit of the Dogcollar Brigade. Mr Bagthorpe by no means wished to conciliate them, but he did want them to know who was the head of his household.

Recriminations were already flying. So completely disunited was the family, that it even appeared that there might be a rift between Grandma and Daisy.

'How *can* you have believed that I should like a dish of maggots?' Grandma asked.

' 'Cos *I* would!' Daisy sobbed. 'I love them, an' I played with them all afternoon and ran them races and things. I nearly kepted them myself. I nearly never gave them to you.'

'Then you should have followed your better judgement and kept them,' Uncle Parker told her, unmoved by this evidence of his daughter's unselfishness.

'Let her be!' cried Aunt Celia. 'Why must Daisy always be blamed?'

'Because, Celia,' Mr Bagthorpe told her, 'Daisy always *is* to blame.'

'She is innocent,' Aunt Celia declared. 'Mother should have accepted the maggots with good grace.'

Mrs Bagthorpe attempted to reintroduce a party spirit by cutting the cake and handing it round, but the only difference this made was that people now shouted and argued with their mouths full. Crumbs flew.

Inevitably those responsible for both smell and maggots

were unmasked. (Mercifully, the existence of the mould among the cress sandwiches and walnut slices was not suspected.) The young Bagthorpes admitted to having produced these things, but did not reveal their motive at the present time.

'We did it for a joke,' William said. 'We thought it'd liven things up a bit.'

'And we didn't mean the maggots for Grandma,' Rosie put in. 'They were stolen. It was Daisy's fault.'

'There. Again the finger points!' cried Aunt Celia.

The row raged on with no sign of abating. Only Jack seemed to notice that Grandpa and Uncle Claud had withdrawn from the fray, and now and again were appearing and trotting across the kitchen bearing trays of dismantled sandwiches and broken dishes. It occurred to him that this was a good thing. Even if the pair of them did notice the mould and fungus, they would be unlikely to remark on it. Jack thought he might help them, to ensure that the incriminating debris had all disappeared before anyone else inspected it. He took advantage of a particularly fiery exchange between Mr Bagthorpe and Aunt Penelope, on the subject of bringing up children at which each maintained the other to be hopeless, to slip out unnoticed.

The smell in the sitting-room was still poisonous even now that all the windows were open. Uncle Claud was on his knees with a dustpan and brush. Grandpa was eating a stuffed egg, in full knowledge that it had been on the floor. Jack was amazed that anyone should find it possible to eat under such circumstances. There the old gentleman sat, quite unperturbed, with a second stuffed egg poised ready to follow the first. Jack knew Grandpa was nearly deaf, but was amazed to find that his sense of smell was also apparently impaired, because he had always understood that if one sense failed, the others became exceptionally acute in compensation.

'Delicious,' Grandpa remarked. 'Mrs Fosdyke stuffs an egg remarkably well. Where *is* Mrs Fosdyke, by the way?'

'Gone,' Jack told him. 'For good, this time, I should think. It's jolly nice of you to clear up, seeing that none of it is your fault.'

'Your Uncle Claud and I are in here because we dislike arguments,' Grandpa told him. 'The smell is bad, certainly, but it is better than an argument.'

He rose and carried on with his self-imposed task, shovelling the pieces of the ginger pot cat into a plastic bucket along with everything else. Later, when Grandma found out that the remains of the replica had been consigned to the dustbin, she became very emotional. It was, she said, a blasphemy and a desecration.

'Someone must retrieve the pieces,' she declared.

'And then what?' inquired Mr Bagthorpe. 'Cremation or burial? Pull one in before you go, can you, Claud?'

'We could dig a real grave,' said Daisy hopefully. She had always regretted missing the funeral of the real Thomas.

Aunt Penelope's lips compressed into virtual invisibility at this irreverent banter, nor was Grandma herself in any mood for it.

'The fact that Thomas was broken at all is an ill omen,' she told them all darkly. 'I believe it was a Sign.'

It was always a bad sign when Grandma started talking about Signs.

'Never mind, Grandma,' Uncle Parker told her. 'I shall get you another. Pronto. Forthwith.'

'It will not be the same,' she told him. 'It could never be the same.'

'You'll never know the difference,' he promised her. Grandma refused to be comforted.

'I shall *know*,' she said obstinately. 'First I lost the original Thomas. Now I have been bereaved of my original replica of him. Any other cat will now be an imposter.'

'It won't,' Uncle Parker assured her. 'Think – it'll be an original replica of the original replica of the original. Try and see it like that.'

Grandma said that she knew she would never be able to see it like that.

'Though you may as well get me another,' she added. 'It will help to remind me of the originals, I suppose, and at least give you some pleasure.'

'Come Claud, come children,' said Aunt Penelope, rising. 'We shall not stay and listen to such frivolity.'

She accordingly swept out, obediently followed by her family. Jack thought frivolity a curious name for what was going on, as did Grandma herself.

'Frivolity indeed!' she snapped. 'That woman is impossible. Has *she* never lost a pot cat?'

'I'm going out to make sure that car of theirs starts,' Mr Bagthorpe said. 'If they remain under this roof another twenty-four hours, I cannot guarantee my sanity.'

The D.B. left immediately after a light breakfast the following morning. It was light partly because nobody had much appetite, and partly because Mrs Fosdyke was not there to prepare it. Mrs Bagthorpe was much worried by this.

'You must go and find out what is the matter,' she told her husband.

'We *know* what is the matter,' he replied. 'Her teeth feel strange.'

'And she may, of course, have been affected adversely by the events of yesterday,' put in Aunt Penelope, 'as indeed I have myself.'

Mr Bagthorpe opened his mouth, then evidently remembered that he had only half an hour more of her company to endure, and closed it again.

'Oh, Fozzy's used to that sort of thing,' William told her. 'It wouldn't be that.'

After breakfast the Dogcollar Brigade went upstairs to say goodbye to Grandma, who had by now so thoroughly lost sight of the Family Reunion aspect of the visit that she had not even bothered to get up to say her farewells. She sat propped up in bed surrounded by her memorophilia of Thomas.

'Come again,' she invited them listlessly, 'once you have reformed your eating habits. And try to get your children shouting, Penelope, before it is too late.'

'Do not forget to listen to the wireless while Luke is becoming Young Brain of Britain,' countered Aunt Penelope. 'And of course we will send you the volume of Esther's poems when it is ready. Perhaps she will inscribe it for you?'

'Oh yes, I will,' Esther confirmed.

'Not with a text, I hope,' said Grandma ungratefully. 'At this house we do not care for texts.'

This was not strictly true. Grandma occasionally had recourse to them herself, but when she did, it was in a very different spirit from that of the Sainted Aunt.

The Bagthorpes gathered on the steps to wave goodbye to their visitors.

'God bless!' called Aunt Penelope magnanimously as the car moved away round the first bend in the drive.

'Keep your fingers crossed,' Mr Bagthorpe told everybody. 'They're still in the drive, yet. If Russell turns in as they turn out, it will be a head on job, this time.'

They waited expectantly, but there was no bang. They let out long breaths of relief and looked at one another with sudden affection. There was nothing like a visit from the D.B. to reinforce their own family feeling, which was never otherwise noticeably strong. All of them, though they would not have admitted this in so many words, were feeling quite well disposed towards one another, and pleased to be the family they were. Even Mr Bagthorpe was temporarily mellowed.

'Well, thank God for that,' he said. 'If you will pardon the expression. They will not be back for a long time.'

Now that the Family Reunion was officially over, the junior Bagthorpes were in a position to concentrate their energies on more serious matters. They did not hold a meeting about these. They had held meetings only while united against a common enemy. From now on, they would operate alone. They were after fame and immortality. They were about to scatter in the pursuit of these elusive goals, when they were prevented by their mother.

'Wait!' she told them.

They hung back impatiently.

'There are the household chores to be done,' she told them.

'I've made my bed,' William said.

'And me,' added Rosie.

'*All* the household chores,' said Mrs Bagthorpe firmly. 'Mrs Fosdyke is evidently not well enough to come in today. And some of the responsibility must, I think, rest with you. She had an extremely trying day yesterday, and you are all partly to blame for this.'

'It's got nothing to do with that,' Rosie objected. 'It's her teeth. We haven't done anything to her teeth.'

'That may well be a psychosomatic symptom of her general malaise,' Mrs Bagthorpe told her. 'It may well be that she will not recover for several days.'

'There may already be a letter in the post,' said Mr Bagthorpe, 'giving in her notice. If she doesn't give it now, I fear she never will.'

'We will draw up a rota of household duties,' Mrs Bagthorpe continued, 'and you yourself, Henry, will have a part to play.'

The atmosphere of general well being and self-congratulation occasioned by the departure of the Latter Day Saints was fast dissipating.

'There is no use my doing anything about the house,' Mr Bagthorpe told her. 'With the best intentions in the world, I should break every electrical labour-saving device within the hour.'

This was probably true. He had a very long record of breaking things. He either broke them, or misused them. On the one occasion he had been entrusted with loading the washing machine, he had set it on the hottest programme and included a brand-new bath towel, so that everything emerged either shrunk, or pale lime, or both.

'I will certainly,' he now conceded generously, 'try to make as little work as possible for the rest of you.'

When Mrs Bagthorpe made clear that this contribution was not acceptable, he followed the others gloomily into the kitchen to oversee the drawing up of the rota. There was still a good backlog of clearing up to do after the previous evening's débâcle, in addition to the routine chores, and it soon became clear that there would be little time left for the pursuit of fame and immortality.

'This family,' observed William with perfect truth, 'is always getting straight out of the fat and into the fire. It's all Hail and Farewell, non-stop. I was going to see how long I could spend beating a tattoo non-stop today.'

'In that case,' said Mr Bagthorpe, 'I suppose that the rest of us must count our blessings. Do not put me down for ironing, Laura, or indeed for anything to do with laundry.'

'When I *do* start my endurance tattoo,' William said, 'I shall need someone to keep bringing me food and liquids, and so forth. The existing record is held by someone from Michigan, and he beat for three hundred and twenty hours.'

'If you start beating a non-stop tattoo,' his father told him, 'there will soon be no living soul left within a mile radius. I do not pretend to know why you should wish to embark on this course, but if ever you do, go somewhere a long way off and do it.'

'He's doing it because he has an inordinate desire for personal aggrandisement,' Tess said jealously. 'I personally do not consider that a tattoo lasting even a full year would prove anything at all.'

She had herself already had the idea of an oboe-playing

marathon, and was considerably put out to find that William had forestalled her.

'As drudgery appears to be the order of the day,' said Mr Bagthorpe, 'I suggest we get started. Where's Mother? What chores is *she* going to do?'

Mrs Bagthorpe hesitated. She had intended exempting both Grandma and Grandpa from duty. On the other hand, she did not wish to antagonize her husband who, though without the remotest sense of justice in the ordinary sense, was a stickler for exact equality in this kind of situation. He was very poor in community spirit.

Mrs Bagthorpe did not herself feel quite up to what would probably be a difficult interview with a still semi-recumbent Grandma. She accordingly sent Jack up, as being the one of her offspring least likely to ruffle Grandma's feelings. He was soon back.

'She says she's busy,' he announced.

'Ha!' Things were playing straight into Mr Bagthorpe's hands. 'Busy, she says. If one were to believe Mother, she is never otherwise, even when asleep.'

This was true. Grandma did have this delusion that she was always busy, and that her life was a ceaseless round of duties and engagements. She would write in her diary the most trivial everyday occurrences, such as 'Go to hair-dresser', and 'Finish reading *The Way of All Flesh*, and Telephone Daisy'. These items were all numbered and listed, and gave the casual onlooker the impression that her life was, indeed, a jetting and frantic affair.

'I doubt,' Mr Bagthorpe had once proclaimed, 'whether the Prime Minister of England has a diary that looks like hers.'

Mrs Bagthorpe tried to stick up for Grandma, saying that she was, after all, quite old, and that when you got to seventy-five perhaps things like purchasing a bar of fruit and nut chocolate and polishing one's nails *did* take on the dimensions of major engagements.

'What she is busy doing,' Mr Bagthorpe now declared, 'is contemplating that horrible dead cat of hers, and casting around for some life-shattering event that will unhinge us all, as did her last one. Whose idea was the Family Reunion? When Armageddon finally comes, it will be Mother who has arranged it.'

'You are exaggerating, Henry,' his wife told him without conviction.

'I shall appoint myself to do the hoovering,' he said. 'And my first act will be to go and hoover Mother's room. I shall drive her thence.'

He departed before anyone could stop him. The rest of them stayed to be allotted tasks that would take them, so far as they could see, the rest of the day, even if thoroughly skimped.

By mid-morning they reassembled in the kitchen for refreshment, and threw themselves into chairs in attitudes of exhaustion.

'We can't keep this up,' William announced. 'We'll have to get Fozzy back.'

'How?' inquired Tess. 'Extract all her teeth, perhaps?'

'Psychology,' William said. 'We exert some psychology. Now, we all know that Fozzy is cussed.'

They did, they agreed.

'You will also have noticed,' he went on, 'that she gets really pleased if anyone butters her up. Look how she smirked when you took those photos of her with her food, Rosie.* And look how chuffed she was yesterday when Mother toasted her.'

* See *Ordinary Jack*.

The others nodded.

'Though I don't see how we're going to photograph her or toast her today,' Jack objected.

'Your trouble,' William told him, 'is that you are too literal. Mrs Fosdyke will receive, within the hour, a large bunch of flowers and a box of chocolates. You go and pick some flowers, Rosie.'

She got up obediently.

'And mind Father doesn't see you,' William warned.

'What about the chocs?' Jack asked. 'Will we all have to fork out?'

'You haven't even got a *memory*,' Wiliam told him. 'There is already a large box of chocolates meant for Fozzy on the sideboard in the sitting-room.'

'So there is.'

Jack recalled now a brief scene from the previous day. It had been a tame scene by yesterday's standards, hence possibly his difficulty in remembering it. Mr Bagthorpe had walked into the sitting-room during the morning and, seeing a large box of chocolates, picked it up and started to pull off the cellophane. The crackling of this had drawn the attention of his wife.

'Stop!' she ordered. 'Those chocolates are for Mrs Fosdyke from all of us, as a token of our appreciation. We shall give them to her straight after the party.'

'With teeth like hers,' Mr Bagthorpe replied, 'I can hardly think of a less tactful gift. And I've pulled the cellophane off now.'

'Never mind,' his wife said, 'the chocolates are still intact. Put them down, Henry.'

'Nobody ever gives me tokens of appreciation,' he said, and put them down with an ill grace.

'So we'll take them down to her,' William told the others.

'And hope to heaven that awful stink hasn't got into them. You can take them, Jack. Fozzy likes you best.'

'Do you think she does?' Jack was unaware that William was subjecting him to the same buttering-up treatment as that being used on Mrs Fosdyke herself. 'All right. I can take Zero. He needs a walk. I'm sure Father's deliberately pushing the hoover at him.'

He set off accordingly some minutes later, bearing a large bouquet of flowers, cunningly wrapped in cellophane to give the impression that it had been removed from the chocolate box for this purpose, and the chocolates themselves.

'Come on, old chap,' he told Zero as they reached the edge of the meadow. 'I'm on an important mission. And you are, as well. Very important. We've been entrusted with it, Zero, old chap. Good boy. Good *boy*.'

And so the pair of them went happily and unwittingly from the fat to the fire.

Chapter 10

It might have been Mrs Fosdyke's imagination that her teeth felt strange, but she obviously thought she was ill in some way, because she was still in her dressing gown and slippers when she opened the door. Jack stuck the bunch of flowers straight out towards her before she could even open her mouth, hoping thus to take the wind out of her sails. This strategy, reasonable as it seemed, failed. Mrs Fosdyke was by now in such a state of nervous agitation and general cosmic insecurity that she jumped back when Jack thrust the flowers at her, evidently supposing that they were about to erupt maggots or poisonous fumes.

'What's them?' she inquired suspiciously.

'They're flowers, Mrs Fosdyke. For you. From all of us. You know – for appreciation and all that.'

Still she seemed not to respond. Jack, realizing why, buried his nose in the flowers to demonstrate their innocuousness.

'There!' he said, coming up for breath. 'Smashing! They smell really nice. Here you are, Mrs Fosdyke.'

She was still unable to bring herself to take the flowers, but held the door a little wider, and said, 'Best come in, I s'pose. Don't s'pose I'm meant to stand in draughts, the state I'm in.'

'I'm sorry about your not being well,' Jack told her truthfully. 'We all are. That's why we've sent the flowers. And these are for you, as well.'

He handed over the box of chocolates. It was large and

handsome, albeit lacking cellophane. Mrs Fosdyke had remarked its presence on the sideboard the previous day, but had assumed it was intended for Grandma. She took it, placed it on the table, and regarded the picture on the lid as if looking for some kind of clue.

'Do you like them?' Jack asked. 'They're a good make. And it's a nice lid.'

'Very nice,' she said at length. She sat down suddenly.

'Just having a cup of tea,' she told him. 'I'll pour you one. Just pass a cup and saucer off that shelf, will you? My legs don't seem up to much today.'

Jack would normally have declined the offer of tea and conversation with Mrs Fosdyke, but felt that today this would be part of his duty as ambassador. Also, he was somewhat alarmed to hear that Mrs Fosdyke's legs were apparently going the same way as her teeth. He probed for further details.

'You were run off your legs yesterday, I expect,' he said, placing his cup and saucer before her.

'I'm always run off my legs,' Mrs Fosdyke told him. 'Nothing new in that. It's their being all of a shock and tremble I don't like.'

'I'm really sorry about your legs, Mrs Fosdyke,' Jack told her. From then on, he kept taking looks to see if he could detect signs of shaking and trembling in her nether limbs. If he could, he supposed it would mean quite a serious illness, like palsy in the Bible. On the other hand, he did not think that the Family Reunion, cataclysmic as it had been, would have been sufficient to bring on the palsy.

'Gone, have they?' inquired Mrs Fosdyke.

Jack, knowing whom she meant, nodded.

'And that's no wonder,' she observed. 'Though mind you, they're not what they were. The Reverend gentleman's nice enough, but now they've all gone on to the vegetables they're not what they were. It makes you wonder if it's something in the blood.'

'What is?' Jack asked, thinking she had gone off at a tangent and was describing another of her symptoms.

'Being a Bagthorpe.'

'Oh.'

Jack did not quite know what to say to this. He did not wish to sit and hear his family maligned, but on the other hand he was very keen to fulfil his mission of buttering up Mrs Fosdyke and getting her back into operation again as soon as possible.

'Why don't you have a chocolate?' he suggested diplomatically.

'I haven't had my breakfast,' she said. 'You don't eat chocolates before breakfast.'

'But it's gone twelve now,' Jack pointed out. 'Even if you haven't had any breakfast, I don't think that gone twelve counts as before breakfast.'

He felt he was handling the debate very well, and Mrs Fosdyke certainly seemed to concede that he had made some kind of point.

'Might as well,' she said. 'What it don't do for my teeth, it might for my legs.'

As it turned out, no chocolate was about to do anything for any part of Mrs Fosdyke's anatomy. Within thirty seconds of the lid of the box being raised, Jack found himself outside the house, the door slammed, and could hear Mrs Fosdyke screaming on the other side.

'Oooooh oooooh oooooooooh!' she screamed, as if she thought that screaming long and loud enough would actually achieve something.

She told her cronies later in the Fiddler's Arms that she had really, at that moment, feared for her own sanity.

'I remember thinking while I was screaming,' she told them, 'that I could *hear* meself screaming, just as if it was somebody else, and I was outside of meself, if you see what I mean.'

Mesdames Bates and Pye nodded sagely and the latter intelligently remarked that this was probably what was meant by the expression 'being beside yourself'.

'That's what you were, Glad,' she told her. 'Beside yourself. It's 'orrible.'

Jack himself reported back to his siblings that he thought Mrs Fosdyke really might be having a nervous breakdown.

'And you can't really blame her,' he said.

His picture of what had happened was only fragmentary, but he had seen the box of chocolates fly up and fall, as if in slow motion, in a shower of large, white maggots.

'They were bigger than the maggots at Grandma's party,' he told them. 'Miles bigger. They must have been eating the chocolates.'

'Gosh!' Rosie was impressed. She had been impressed by the orginal maggots.

'There's no need to ask who *put* 'em there, of course,' William said grimly.

There was not. They could all well imagine what had, in fact, happened, and this was later confirmed by Daisy herself.

'I di'n't *want* all the dear little maggots to die of that horrid smell,' she sobbed. 'I saved them.'

She had eaten six of the chocolates, she said, to make room for her salvaged pets.

'It made all little nice nests where the chocolates were,' she told them. 'They looked really comfy.'

She then swiftly reversed the situation by demanding accusingly:

'Why did you give my maggots to Mrs Fozzy? They were *my* maggots. I saved them. Now I haven't got *no* maggots.'

'You're crazy,' William told her. 'Hopeless. I ask you!'

Daisy began to sob afresh, and Rosie rounded on William

and Tess – the latter having been equally scathing about Daisy's humane treatment of the maggots.

'Shut *up*!' she told them. 'Leave her alone. She's sweet. She only meant to be kind. It was your fault, sending Fozzy those chocolates. *You* weren't trying to be kind. You were just trying to get her back to do all the work, and now she won't come back, not ever, and it'll serve you right!'

This speech had a sobering effect, if only because it contained the now patent truth that Mrs Fosdyke was indeed unlikely ever to cross the Bagthorpe threshold again.

'Mother'll just have to find someone else,' Tess said at last.

'She won't be able to,' Jack said. 'Fozzy tells tales about us in the village. She makes out we're awful. And mad.'

'That's true,' Tess conceded. 'Mother would have to advertise nationally, and get someone who has never heard of us.'

'Which won't be easy,' William pointed out, 'considering all the adverse publicity we've been getting lately.'

They moodily turned the matter over in their heads.

'There's only one thing,' William said at last. 'We'll have to make a final bid to get Fozzy back.'

'You can,' Jack told him. 'I'm not.'

'She does like us, in a way,' William continued. 'She must, or she wouldn't have stayed as long as she has. The first thing is, Daisy must write a letter of apology.'

Daisy stopped sniffing and brightened up.

'Shall I write on the wall you mean?' she asked.

'You write on a wall,' William told her, 'and I'll skin you alive. You write a proper letter on proper paper, and in your best writing.'

'Yes, Willum,' said Daisy meekly.

Rosie was ordered to take Daisy off, give her some paper,

and stand over her while she wrote the letter. Half an hour later, Daisy reappeared triumphantly waving her missive.

It read:

Dear Miz Fozzy I am sorry you got my magots in your choclots and please can I have them back becos I reely love them and can play with them insted of bruthers and sisters becos mummy says I can't have anny bruthers and sisters. I hop your teef is beter and we al reely and trully luv you we reely do and reely meen it that we luv you.

Daisy.

William cast a weary eye over this communication and said that in his view it contained far too much of the word 'reely', which sounded, he said, like protesting too much. Jack pointed out that it would look even worse if the protestations of love were struck out, and it was decided that the letter should stand.

'Though *that* won't fetch Fozzy back,' Jack told them. 'You didn't see the size of those maggots, and you didn't hear her screeching. It'll take more than that.'

'If we are ever to win fame,' William said, 'and I mean *quick* fame, before the D.B. do, we must *think* of something more than that.'

They all thought, with the possible exception of Daisy, who did not really appreciate the seriousness of the situation, and was probably still thinking about maggots. She announced her intention of going up to see Grandma, whom Mr Bagthorpe had not managed to hoover out of her room.

'What *would* make Fozzy happy, in the whole world?' Jack wondered out loud.

They pondered in silence. Mrs Fosdyke did not talk a lot about happiness. They did not, they realized, know what was her dearest wish, even were they able to grant it.

'I don't think she ever *gets* actually happy.' Jack was voicing the thought of them all.

'The only time she looked really happy,' Rosie said, 'was when I took those photos of her with my birthday food. She even comes out happy on the photos.'

'Let's think around that,' William said.

They accordingly sat and thought around that.

'There's one thing certain,' William remarked, 'there's no point in suggesting another party, even if you took a thousand photos of her and her stuffed eggs.'

They all took this point. The word 'party' was clearly to be avoided at all costs.

'She might like to be *immortal*,' Rosie suggested. 'I mean, we're all going to try and be immortal, and I think most people would like to be, if they could.'

'Her? Immortal?' William let out a fair copy of one of his father's sardonic laughs.

'I don't see why not,' Jack said. As one unlikely ever to win immortality himself, as one of the great, silent majority of the irretrievably ordinary, he felt bound to stand up and be counted with Mrs Fosdyke.

'And in any case,' Tess said thoughtfully, 'she doesn't actually have to *be* immortal. She merely has to be under the impression that she will be. And there is one way she'd think that.'

They all looked hopefully at her.

'A portrait,' she said. 'Rosie could do her portrait.'

'Oh *no*!' Rosie cried. 'Not *her*!'

'Why not?' Tess asked. 'You can do anybody, Rosie, if you really try. You did Grandma. I think that if you could do Grandma, you could do anybody.'

'The only thing is,' Jack said, 'that Rosie's Portraits do

seem to be a bit doomed. I mean, they're jolly good, but they do seem to trigger things off.'

'They do *not*!' squeaked Rosie indignantly.

The others, however, knew that Jack had made a pertinent point. Rosie's Portraits often went the same way as Bagthorpe parties. Even the impressive Portrait of Grandma had been achieved only after two previous abortive attempts, one of which had gone up in flames, and the other been trampled on by Rosie herself. Mrs Fosdyke knew about this, and would almost certainly regard an invitation to sit for Rosie with the profoundest suspicion.

'She would be torn,' Tess said, 'between vanity and terror. We must put the proposition to her, and pray that vanity wins the day.'

'But where could I do her?' Rosie objected. 'The dining-room's all burnt up and the sitting-room smells and I'm not doing her outside. People's faces don't look interesting when they're outside.'

'You can do her in the kitchen,' William told her. 'Where else? She could make some meringues, or something, and you could put those in as well. It'd be an added inducement.'

All in all, this scheme seemed the best they could come up with. They realized that the bait was by no means irresistible, and managed to add a few extras by way of further incentive. In the attic they found a large gilt frame surrounding an oil painting of some depressed-looking Highland cattle. This was in the attic because nobody could stand to look at it, and it had come out only once in the last twenty years, to cover one of Daisy's mottoes when she had been in her Writing on Walls Phase. They took their mother into their confidence about the plot to lure Mrs Fosdyke back to Unicorn House, and obtained her consent to remove the painting from the frame. Mrs Bagthorpe was at least as keen as anyone else to retain the services of Mrs Fosdyke, because her whole future as Stella Bright seemed to depend upon it.

'If Fozzy's going to be framed,' William said with satisfaction, 'she might as well be framed properly. If we take this down with us and show it to her, she'll think she's going to be an instant Old Master. It'll tip the balance, you'll see.'

They decided that they would all visit Mrs Fosdyke that afternoon, with the exception of Daisy, who would be represented by her missive. Mr Bagthorpe, when he was appraised of the situation, was pessimistic about its outcome.

'She'll never sit,' he told them. 'She never sits. And even if she does, the buns'll begin to burn in the middle, or the stew stick, or whatever, and the whole pantomime'll start all over again.'

When challenged to suggest a better plan for luring Mrs Fosdyke back to the house, he was unable to do so.

'And if she doesn't come,' William told him, 'you won't get much script-writing done.'

Mr Bagthorpe quietened down after this, contenting himself with saying that he hoped Rosie would have the good sense to make the likeness flattering. A true likeness, he said, would send Mrs Fosdyke's teeth into a galloping decline. It would also have the effect of a Medusa's head on other people.

'Lop a couple of inches off her nose,' he advised, 'and try to get her looking human, if you can.'

Straight after lunch the young Bagthorpes set off across the meadow to the village, taking turns to carry the large frame in pairs. When Mrs Fosdyke came to her door, she opened it only a crack, which seemed to indicate that she, like Aunt Celia, had totally lost her sense of Cosmic Security.

'Now what?' she snapped ungraciously. 'You're bad,

wicked children, you are. How children ever got to be so unfeeling and persecuting I'll never know. And what're you doing with that great thing?'

'Look, Mrs Fosdyke,' said William, who had been appointed spokesman because, he claimed, he knew how to be tactful. 'We're really sorry about that box of chocolates. We solemnly swear that we gave them in absolute good faith. And we can prove it. Can we come in?'

Mrs Fosdyke looked uncertain.

'We swear we haven't got any maggots,' Rosie said. 'Ough!' – as Tess kicked her ankle. It had been previously agreed that certain loaded words, such as party, anniversary, fire, flood and maggots, were to be totally eschewed during the forthcoming interview. They would act, William said, as triggers, and send Mrs Fosdyke into an immediate decline. He was evidently right about that, because she let out a little scream, and cried:

'Don't talk about it! Don't talk about it!'

'We won't,' William promised. 'Can we come in, then?'

After a hesitation she reluctantly held the door open and they passed through in silence. Jack noticed that the bunch of flowers was still lying where she had put them on the table. Mrs Fosdyke had evidently suspected them of being booby-trapped. He could not help feeling that this was sad.

'We have brought a letter of sincere apology from Daisy, Mrs Fosdyke,' began Tess without preamble. 'It was Daisy who was solely responsible for the ma – unfortunate episode involving the chocolates.'

'Little madam her!' Mrs Fosdyke took the envelope and ripped it open with a ferocity that was a good sign, really. Her attention was now focused on something other than her own teeth and legs.

The Bagthorpes waited in silence while Mrs Fosdyke ran her eye over Daisy's letter of propitiation.

'Have them back!' she exclaimed. 'Ugh! Brothers and sisters indeed. What that little madam wants *is* brothers and sisters, let alone maggots. Love indeed!'

She did, none the less, look marginally gratified. Evidently Daisy's lavish use of the word 'reely' was making the desired impression.

'We're all sorry, of course,' William told her, pressing home the advantage. 'And we've been racking our brains to think how we can make it up to you.'

'What do you think of this, Mrs Fosdyke?' Tess gestured towards the heavy gilt frame which was propped against Mrs Fosdyke's formica sink unit, looking very out of place and exotic. Mrs Fosdyke eyed it with hostility and suspicion.

'What's that meant to be for, then?' she demanded. 'Seen that before, I have, I reckon. Where's the middle gone out of it, then?'

'The picture it was framing,' said William swiftly, 'which was an extremely rare and valuable one of Highland Cattle in Scotch Mist, has been removed and sacrificed to make way for a more worthwhile and interesting subject.'

'Ooooh, yes!' Mrs Fosdyke's brow cleared. 'That's it. It was them horrible cows out the attic. Does your ma know?'

'Mother is absolutely in favour,' Tess assured her. 'She feels that the frame could not be put to a better use. So does Father.'

'What use?' Mrs Fosdyke was still on the defensive.

'What we all think,' said William carefully, aware that the crux of the interview was approaching, 'is that Rosie should paint your Portrait.'

There was a silence.

'For posterity,' Tess added.

'To make you immortal,' Jack explained. 'When you have your Portrait done, you get immortal.'

Mrs Fosdyke had evidently never given much thought to the matter of her own immortality. She did not seem even quite to understand what was being offered to her.

Jack, seeing this, attempted a further elucidation.

'It means,' he told her, 'that you'll still be there even when you're dead.'

William scowled at him.

'Dead?' echoed Mrs Fosdyke. 'Who said anything about dead? You don't die of your teeth, so far as I know, or your legs. I never heard anything so downright morbid.'

Jack realizing his *faux pas*, tried to remedy the situation.

'Even *I'm* going to die one day, Mrs Fosdyke,' he said. 'We all are. Rosie is, even Zero is. That's why everybody ought to have their portrait painted. That's why me and Zero did.'

'And in your case,' William went on smoothly, 'we thought that an ordinary frame would be out of the question. We thought this one would be ideal.'

'Hmmmm.' Mrs Fosdyke favoured it with an appraising stare. 'Like an Old Master, kind of, like there was in this big stately home place we went to with the W.I.'

'Exactly!' William shot a triumphant look at the others. 'It would be like a Dutch Master of the Interior School. Rosie'd do you in the kitchen. With all your masterpieces – you know, pork pies and gateaux and such.'

'We – ell...' Mrs Fosdyke was succumbing. 'Them photos came out a treat, all right.' She gestured to the wall where hung the three photographs of herself with Rosie's birthday food.

'I'd do a really good portrait, Mrs Fosdyke,' Rosie promised. 'I think you'd be a really good subject. You've got an interesting face.'

Mrs Fosdyke had never been told this before. She patted her hair deprecatingly.

'When was you thinking of doing it?' she inquired. 'I'd had in mind to stop off the rest of the week. What with one thing and another.'

What she had really had in mind, was to sit down and write a letter giving her notice. It now seemed to her that this would have been over-reacting to what was, after all, not so extreme an occurrence by Bagthorpian standards.

'The thing is,' said Rosie, who had been primed for this eventuality, 'that I'm in an Inspired Phase at the moment. Sometimes I get more inspired than usual, and that's how I am at the moment. If I could start on your Portrait tomorrow I think it could easily be the best I've ever done. Better than Grandma's, even.'

'Could it really?' Mrs Fosdyke was clearly impressed.

'Yes, honestly,' Rosie said.

It was very gallant of her, Jack thought. She had not the least desire to spend hours cooped up in the kitchen struggling to catch the likeness of a smirking Mrs Fosdyke. In actual fact, she said, she thought Mrs Fosdyke unpaintable.

'Well, p'raps I ought, then,' Mrs Fosdyke said. 'And particular when you've gone to all that trouble taking them cows out of that frame. Worth hundreds of pound, that frame, I daresay.'

Mrs Fosdyke had a notoriously inflated idea of the value of the Bagthorpe's possessions, and had once told her cronies in the Fiddler's Arms that the family were probably, in her opinion, millionaires. When the Portrait was completed, and framed, and dominating her own tiny overcrowded lounge, there was little doubt that Mesdames Pye and Bates would be invited round to view it. Most of the village would, in time.

'You'll come then?' William asked. 'Tomorrow?'

Mrs Fosdyke nodded.

'I shall go and get my hair done this afternoon,' she said, 'and I'll be round in the morning, usual time.'

The Bagthorpes let out concerted sighs of relief. The day was won, the Highland Cattle had been well lost, and Mrs Fosdyke was to be framed and hung.

Chapter 11

Mrs Bagthorpe praised her children highly when she heard that Mrs Fosdyke was to resume her duties the following day. Mr Bagthorpe greeted the news with a tempered enthusiasm. While prepared to admit that the household would run more smoothly than it had in her absence, he nonetheless thought the Portrait for Posterity foolhardy and ill-considered.

'Once hung in gilt she will become impossible,' he predicted. 'And she will probably demand a rise in her wages.'

The kitchen during the next few days certainly was to become more than usually Mrs Fosdyke's exclusive territory, and this meant one fewer place of refuge for the Bagthorpes, already without a dining- and sitting-room. Mrs Fosdyke was very keen that the background to her Portrait should be right, and kept cooking mouth-watering things that she would not allow to be consumed until they had been immortalized in paint. Accordingly much pressure was put on Rosie to get the Portrait done as quickly as possible, but this she refused to do. This Portrait was by far the largest yet commissioned, and she herself was unaccustomed to being framed in nineteenth-century gilt. Furthermore, Rosie well knew that her siblings had already started on their relentless pursuit of glory, and felt that if she could achieve a deathless Portrait of Mrs Fosdyke she would at least be level-pegging.

'I shall send it to the National Portrait Gallery,' she told everyone.

'What for?' inquired William.

William, as eldest, felt that it was important that he should achieve immortality sooner than any of the others. He was determined to carry through his idea of a non-stop tattoo, but was wanting an assistant. Clearly he would have to remain in his own room with the door shut, and equally clearly he would need sustenance during the long and arduous performance. Three hundred and twenty-one hours was a long time. Nobody wanted to volunteer to bring his meals up to him.

'You'll have to take a bowl of fruit up,' Tess told him. 'That should at least keep you alive. Gandhi frequently lasted on less.'

William, unwilling to undergo this kind of deprivation, even in the interests of immortality, was reduced to suggesting to Grandma that Daisy be invited to stay for a few days. He in no way admired or trusted Daisy, but knew that the idea of trotting regularly up to the top floor bearing trays of food would appeal to her. Grandma said that she would love to have Daisy to stay as long as she did not bring any maggots. William explained that the last of the maggots had gone to Mrs Fosdyke, and Grandma accordingly telephoned The Knoll and invited Daisy. After some persuasion from Uncle Parker, Aunt Celia reluctantly agreed, with the proviso that Daisy should be allowed to do exactly as she wished, and should not be spoken to harshly. Grandma readily agreed to these conditions, and went to tell the rest of the household about Daisy's forthcoming visit. The reception of this intelligence ranged from the lukewarm to the frigid. Mr Bagthorpe was absolutely against it, and said that Daisy was a bad influence on Grandma.

'Mother is too old, and too impressionable, to be exposed to such company,' he declared.

Even Mrs Bagthorpe was dubious. The following day

decorators were due to begin work on the burnt-out dining-room, and she was hoping that this time the colour scheme would be of her own choosing. The one good thing that had come out of the Christmas Day fire was that the toad-coloured walls perpetrated by the indefatigable Daisy* were now to be painted eau de nil, as had been originally intended.

'I must warn the decorators,' she said worriedly, 'and myself ensure that all tins of paint are kept tightly closed.'

Mrs Fosdyke requested that Daisy be kept out of the kitchen. Her attitude toward Daisy had softened since the letter of apology, but she was in no way convinced that Daisy's character had undergone any permanent change.

'The leopard don't change his stripes,' she said darkly, 'and nor will *she* have.'

'She will come to the kitchen only for her meals,' Mrs Bagthorpe promised. 'And we must try not to be too hard on her. She is, after all, only just five.'

'And getting older every day,' returned Mrs Fosdyke. 'More's the pity.'

Tess, who would be spending most of her time holed up in her room, was not against the visit, though she would have been had she known the real reason for it. She thought Daisy was coming merely to keep Grandma company, and as yet knew nothing of the part she was to play in the marathon tattoo.

What Tess intended to do was to write out the Collected Works of Voltaire by hand in a record time. She did not know what the existing record time was, and it occurred to her that perhaps one did not exist. This did not deter her.

'If no one has done it before,' she thought, 'then my record will stand until someone breaks it.'

*See *Absolute Zero*.

She wrote off a letter to the *Guinness Book of Records* appraising them of her intended feat, and informing them that the French teacher at her school would undertake to supervise. He had thought the idea a very good one, and said it would bring Tess's French on even further. Mr Bagthorpe, on the other hand, said that in his opinion Tess would end up by thinking she *was* Voltaire, and probably have to be committed to an asylum.

By now Mr Bagthorpe knew what his brood were about, and why. He was in favour, in principle, of his own offspring outshining those of the Sainted Aunt, but wished they could do it more quickly and quietly.

'What you are lacking in,' he told them, 'is careless ease. There's altogether too much striving after effect.'

The only one of the younger Bagthorpes not now striving after effect was Jack, who thought his chances of attaining immortality infinitesimal.

'In any case, old chap,' he told Zero, 'immortality is in a grain of sand, and in any case, you are immortal. You're already immortal. You're a household word. And if Rosie sends Fozzy's Portrait to the National Gallery, I'll get her to send ours as well.'

As soon as Daisy arrived the next day, William took her aside and explained to her what he wanted.

'I am going to be in the *Guinness Book of Records*,' he told her, 'and you can have the honour of helping me.'

'Oh *sank* you, Willum!' she cried. 'Can *I* bang on some dums?'

'Not now, Daisy,' he told her, 'but you can have a go when I've finished. What I want you to do, is to bring my meals up to me on a tray. You can pretend to be a waitress.'

'Is that a good thing to be?' she asked. 'A waitress?'

'A very good thing,' he assured her.

'Will I get tired?' she asked. 'I'm only little, and I might get tired. Or I might forget.'

'You'll have to be really grown-up,' he said, 'and try to remember.'

Daisy pondered the matter. Evidently the idea of being a waitress did not appeal to her so strongly as he had hoped it might. She was, after all, used to doing things much more exciting than going back and forth up long flights of stairs with trays.

'If I *did* forget,' she mused, 'I 'spect you'd starve.'

'Yes, I would,' William said, in the mistaken belief that this would force her into an affirmative decision.

'If you *did* starve,' she went on, more or less to herself, 'you'd get thinner and thinner and shrink and shrink and in the end you'd be just bones. I've seen someone who was just bones, and he was called a skelington and he was dead.'

Even now William failed to see the warning signals.

'That's quite right, Daisy,' he told her solemnly. 'So you see what an important job you'll be doing. It's a matter of life and death.'

This stark summary of the position clinched the matter.

'I don't sink I will, sank you, Willum,' she said politely. 'You see, I only ever seen *one* skelington and I never even saw him properly. And when *you're* a skelington I can come and look at your bones really properly. And I can write a pome about them.'

William cursed inwardly, and would dearly have liked to make Daisy herself a candidate for an elegy. He did not, however, as a Bagthorpe, give up. He had a sudden inspiration.

'I bet you were really upset when you lost all your maggots,' he said.

Daisy nodded sadly.

'I was. I cried. I cried so much I thought Mummy would get me some more, but she wouldn't, and Daddy wouldn't either.'

'I don't expect they could,' he told her. 'You need magic to make maggots, Daisy, and there's only really me knows how to do it.'

'Mazic?' Daisy's eyes widened, and William saw that he had made a breakthrough. The combination of magic and maggots was going to prove irresistible.

'Can you mazic maggots, Willum?'

'I *could*,' he said. 'It would depend.'

Daisy caught his drift instantly. He was using a technique she sometimes used herself, having been taught it by Grandma.

'I will fetch the trays, Willum,' she said, 'and I really will try and remember. Can I have a *lot* of maggots? Can I have them now?'

'Not now,' he said. 'It's not instant magic. But I'll make them as soon as I can, I promise.'

The deal was thus sealed, and William set for his record-breaking attempt. He fetched some cold meat and set it in the airing cupboard to produce Daisy's eventual reward. At lunch he announced to his family that this would be the last meal he would be taking with them for some time. He also handed his mother a statement:

I, Laura Fay Bagthorpe, hereby certify that my son, William Magnus Bagthorpe, is undertaking a world-record-breaking attempt for the longest drum tattoo under my own strict supervision. I certify that this tattoo commenced at 1400 hours 5th April, and ended...
Rests of fifteen minutes every three hours will be taken.

'Under my strict supervision?' queried Mrs Bagthorpe. 'Am I to stay up all night to supervise?'

'If he is allowed to go through with this,' said Mr Bagthorpe, 'and I myself categorically forbid it, we shall *all* be up all night.'

'Oh, I think we should let him, dear,' said his wife. 'We have always agreed that the children should be allowed to extend themselves in every possible way.'

'I shouldn't think he'll last until much past tea-time anyway,' Tess said jealously. 'In fact the regular rhythm of the beat will probably send him into a hypnotic trance long before that. He may not even be able to get out of it again.'

Mrs Bagthorpe was alarmed by this prospect.

'Try to beat *irregularly*, dear,' she told William.

'I can't,' he replied. 'You've got to have a rhythm.'

'In that case,' Mr Bagthorpe prophesied, 'you will emerge from your room a whirling dervish. And those of us who have been within earshot will ourselves become whirling dervishes, and God knows how it will all end.'

William left the table and approached Mrs Fosdyke, who was at the sink making a rattle sufficiently subdued to allow her to hear the conversation.

'Do you think I could have two thermos flasks of coffee?' he asked. 'I shall need them during the night.'

'Luckily,' she replied, 'I can't hear the row you make on them drums when I'm in my kitchen, and praise be I don't sleep here, neither. You can have coffee for me, if your ma don't mind.'

Mrs Bagthorpe, who thought that strong coffee might minimize the chance of William going into a trance or becoming a whirling dervish, gave her consent. William, then, armed with his flasks, a bag of fruit and a large bar of fruit and nut chocolate, went up to the top storey to begin his endurance test.

'Good luck!' Jack called after him. He thought the rest of the family were being unnecessarily dismissive about William's record-breaking attempt.

A few minutes later they all heard the distant throbbing of the drums. They were less than usually audible because William had decided that he would beat his tattoo fairly gently, the better to conserve his strength.

'What a totally unproductive performance,' remarked Tess, still chafing at having been forestalled.

'If that row goes on much longer,' said Mr Bagthorpe, 'I shall be rendered totally non-productive.'

'Nonsense, Henry,' his wife said. 'One can hardly hear the drums at all.'

'You are not a sensitive creative writer,' he told her. 'I have antennae that pick up vibrations like a hoover sucks up dust. If the vibrations in my study go to pot, I shall go up and break his drums over his head.'

Tess left to begin her copying of Voltaire. She telephoned her French teacher and told him she was about to begin. Jack, feeling that the task she had set herself was one of truly shattering monotony, wished her luck, too.

'At least I shall not be wasting my time, even if I do not establish a record,' she said.

Rosie, feeling threatened by the determined efforts of the other two, asked Mrs Fosdyke if she would sit for a while after lunch.

'The light will be better than in the mornings,' she told her, 'and make you look younger.'

'It's lovely to see you all setting your sights on immortality,' Mrs Bagthorpe said. 'Have you thought of what you will do yet, Jack?'

'No, I haven't,' he said. 'I don't need to. Zero and me are bracketed together, and he's already immortal.'

'So, of course, are Daisy and myself,' interposed Grandma.

'Bilge, Mother,' returned her son. 'You and Daisy are appearing on the screen at ever-lengthening intervals, probably because people are now brushing their teeth with Blue Lagoon Toilet Soap and foaming at the mouth.'

Grandma, although she would not admit it, knew this to be true. Daisy and herself had made two near-identical sets of commercials, one for soap and one for toothpaste. Grandma had even worn the same dress and earrings. Neither of the companies concerned had been very pleased when this fact emerged, particularly as they had believed their commercials to be highly original, and had paid out large cash prizes to Grandma and Daisy. It was unlikely that the Unholy Alliance would ever again be used in commercials, and their star was already in the descendant.

'Come along, Daisy dear,' Grandma said, rising. 'We will go up to my room and see what can be done. If I am ever at a loss, I like to talk to Thomas.'

'Like me and my maggots,' agreed Daisy, trotting after her. 'And like me and Arry Awk.'

'Arry Awk?' Grandma stopped dead in her tracks. 'I thought, Daisy, that we had heard the last of that dreadful person. Where is he, and what has he been doing?'

'It was his idea to put the maggots in Mrs Fozzy's box,' Daisy said. 'Arry Awk likes maggots, as well.'

'Run along, Daisy, there's a good girl,' said Mrs Bagthorpe hastily.

She wanted as little talk of maggots as possible at the present time, while Mrs Fosdyke was still in a critical phase. She herself was not much cheered by the intelligence that

Arry Awk was again in the offing. He, Grandma and Daisy made a formidable, if not invincible, trio. The only comfort was that Grandma did not like Arry Awk, and was jealous of his place in Daisy's affections. Perhaps, Mrs Bagthorpe told herself encouragingly, Grandma would see off Arry Awk before he got a chance to do very much.

Mr Bagthorpe, however, took the precaution of telephoning the Parkers and warning them that they must take sole responsibility for any outrages perpetrated by Arry Awk during Daisy's visit.

'I want a signed statement from you, Russell, first thing in the morning,' Jack heard him say. 'And why your daughter cannot find friends of her own age, and visible to the human eye, is a mystery to me. The child consorts only with old women, invisible entities and maggots. If I had the misfortune to be her father, this would disturb me profoundly. I have recommended a visit to a psychiatrist more times than I care to remember, but you are obviously bent on postponing this until it is too late.'

Jack did not know what Uncle Parker said in return, but it must have been something typically infuriating, because Mr Bagthorpe then shouted:

'And if that accursed infant is not conclusive proof of the effects of heredity and environment, I should like to know what is!' and slammed down the receiver. He then went into his study and banged the door.

Unicorn House seemed suddenly depressingly deserted and quiet. Even the muffled sound of drums from above was already becoming as familiar and unnoticeable as the ticking of a clock. No sound came from the kitchen, where Rosie was painting Mrs Fosdyke in the flattering afternoon light. Mrs Bagthorpe was upstairs being Stella Bright.

'I'll tell you what, old chap,' Jack told Zero. 'I hope Arry

Awk *does* do something. It's going to be pretty boring for people like you and me, who're already immortal, sitting round waiting for other people to be.'

Zero grunted, and opened his eyes marginally. Even he seemed to have gone preternaturally quiet.

'P'raps it's the calm before the storm,' Jack thought hopefully. He went upstairs and began to carry on the construction of his model glider, which would never, he knew, make him immortal, but might, with any luck, eventually fly.

Chapter 12

Things began to go drastically wrong sooner even than Jack could have hoped.

Hardly anyone went to bed in a very good mood that night (and William, of course, did not go to bed at all). Rosie was dissatisfied with her Portrait, and wondering whether her first instinct, that Mrs Fosdyke was unpaintable, had not been the right one. Tess had by ten o'clock transcribed only thirty-four out of a total of two thousand and ninety-four pages of Voltaire, and had writer's cramp. Mrs Bagthorpe had not been able to concentrate on her Problems for worrying about the possibility of William's either going into an irreversible trance or emerging at any moment as a whirling dervish. Mr Bagthorpe had been unable to concentrate on his script because he maintained that William's tattoo was already beginning to 'build up', as he described it, in his study.

'My own brain has already become as a skin drum,' he declared. 'And in the night my subconscious mind will be insidiously invaded. The very citadel of my creativity is under attack.'

He was so constantly asserting, without supporting evidence, that he was about to dry up for ever as a writer, that none of the family took much notice of this. They felt he was at least as well off as they were themselves. The only members of the household who had retired in good humour (Jack himself was in a neutral state of mind) were Grandma and Daisy. This in itself was hardly an encouraging sign for the rest of them, as the Unholy Alliance tended to appear at its most benign when at its most destructive.

'Daisy and I will set about becoming immortal tomorrow,' Grandma told them all. '*Doubly* immortal, I should say. We have hit upon a most symbolic and poetic way of doing so.'

Even Mrs Bagthorpe did not much like the sound of this. The last time Daisy had been poetic and symbolic, the entire house had had to be redecorated.

'With Arry Awk helping?' she inquired anxiously.

'Certainly not,' replied Grandma promptly.

'He might,' Daisy said. 'If I need him, I'll ask him.'

'You leave him out of it,' Mr Bagthorpe advised her. 'You realize, don't you, that you are on the verge of bankrupting your father?'

'Hush, Henry,' his wife said. 'Remember what we promised Celia.'

'I made no promises to anyone,' he said. 'Mother did all the promising. And even she was not aware at the time that we should also be entertaining Arry Awk, I believe?'

'Any friend of Daisy's is a friend of mine,' said Grandma obstinately. She wholeheartedly detested Arry Awk, and was extremely jealous of him, but she did not wish to risk alienating Daisy, and in any case liked to needle her son whenever possible.

'I'm taking William his sausages,' Daisy then announced. 'So he doesn't get into a skelington.'

With this she left the room, and returned a few minutes later with a request for two large slices of cake. Mr Bagthorpe was against this being granted.

'It might be our only chance,' he said, 'to starve him out.'

Daisy, however, insisted.

'I'm going to get a secret if I do it,' she said.

The cake was therefore sent up, arriving, however, a little frayed around the edges, where Daisy informed an accusatory William, Arry Awk had been nibbling at it.

When Jack awoke the following morning, the first thing he noticed was that the drums had stopped. His room was directly beneath William's, and on one or two occasions during the night he had awoken and been momentarily aware of the throb of drums overhead. He even remembered having wondered whether Zero might be affected by this, with his having such an acute sense of hearing.

The next thing Jack became conscious of was voices raised to a pitch remarkable even by Bagthorpian standards. Picking up his clock, he saw that the time was just before seven. Zero was still asleep. A particularly high-pitched burst of screaming from Daisy brought Jack leaping out of bed and on to the landing. Here was taking place a full-scale confrontation between Bagthorpes in various stages of undress. William and Mr Bagthorpe were both in their pyjamas, and both shouting. Daisy, clinging to Grandma's nightdress, was sobbing bitterly. Rosie was trying to make her own voice heard above the others and Mrs Bagthorpe, her hair in madly swinging plaits, was vainly trying to arbitrate – or referee.

'Sixteen hours!' Jack heard William shout.

'Don't talk to me about sixteen hours!' yelled Mr Bagthorpe. '*I* know how long it's been! And for God's sake stop shouting!'

'It serves you right!' screamed Rosie. 'Daisy's only little. You're a bully, a great, horrible bully!'

In a miraculous hiatus, which could have occurred only by everyone present simultaneously pausing to draw breath, Grandma said coldly:

'I think I know a storm in a teacup when I see one. Come, Daisy, we will have no part in it. We have our own affairs to attend to.'

With this she withdrew into her room, taking Daisy with her, and closed the door.

Mrs Bagthorpe took advantage of the resulting stunned silence to say, with an attempt at cheerfulness:

'Come along, everybody! Let's go down to the kitchen and make coffee and talk about the whole thing sensibly.'

They went down to the kitchen and made coffee, but practically nobody talked sensibly. It was some time before everyone present had a clear picture of what it was they were all shouting about. What *had* happened emerged only gradually, partly because just as everyone was beginning to calm down, Grandma and Daisy reappeared. Grandma could never resist a row.

'Daisy has confided in me what part she played in this ridiculous charade,' she announced, 'and her case must be represented. I will not tolerate her being slandered in her absence.'

What had happened, then, was this.

Fact the First

William, having been conscientiously beating his tattoo through the long, lonely hours of the night, had hit bottom around dawn. He had run out of food and drink, he said, and was feeling faint. He had not felt that his mother would want to find him lying unconscious in his room when she came up to investigate, and had stopped his tattoo while he decided on his best course of action.

Fact the Second

As he sat thus faintly ruminating, Daisy had poked her head into the room. (Daisy was a notoriously early riser, a fact that Aunt Celia attributed to an over-powerful brain, but about which the Bagthorpes had their own theories.) She had inquired why he had stopped drumming, and on being told the reason, had offered to fetch food and drink. William had considered this proposition, but turned it down. He had not, he explained, thought it either wise or public-spirited to give Daisy the unsupervised freedom of the kitchen or pantry.

'She might have set fire to it or flooded it,' he said, 'or mixed everything together to make an explosion.'

Grandma instantly objected to this, and ruled it out of order.

'That is mere supposition,' she told William. 'You are alleging a purely hypothetical crime. You are leading the jury. Kindly limit yourself to the facts.'

(Sometimes Grandma found her addiction to television police serials paid off handsomely.)

At this Mr Bagthorpe pointed out that the present jury was hopelessly prejudiced anyway, and any false hopes of fair play or justice could be ruled out right away.

William had thought, he continued, that he owed it to his mother to go down and get food, even though he realized that this might take longer than the fifteen minutes' authorized break.

'And you hoped nobody would know!' Rosie cried. 'You thought we were all asleep and wouldn't hear, and you were *cheating*!'

'I was doing nothing of the sort,' he retorted. 'I was jeopardizing my chance of a record, certainly, but I hoped to be back at my drums within fifteen minutes.'

'Oh, you *fibber*!'

Rosie jumped up and fetched the frying pan and brandished it under his nose, thereby splashing warm fat over her mother.

'You were frying bacon and egg. We can *smell* it. We're not deaf, you know!'

William went very red and tried to bluster his way out of the situation by saying he had realized that the fry-up would take too long, and snatched up some bread and marmalade instead.

'Where, in that case, is the bacon?' cried Grandma triumphantly. As Defence Counsel, she felt she had him here.

'And what we're talking about,' he went on, using the time-honoured tactic of attacking as the best form of defence, 'isn't what I had to eat, but what happened to my *drums*.'

Fact the Third

Daisy, when William declared his intention of going downstairs to forage for food, pleaded to be allowed to continue the tattoo in his absence. To this request William had replied with a firm negative. Having no real reason to trust Daisy, he had taken the precaution of bearing the drumsticks away with him, thus thinking to render her helpless.

Daisy, however, was not thus easily rendered helpless.

Fact the Fourth

Daisy at first contented herself with fingering the drums – in itself a new experience, because William, as a rule, would allow her nowhere near them. Her initial curiosity satisfied, she then tried to beat out a little rhythm with her fingers.

'I was trying to do *John Brown's Body*,' she told them, 'but my fingers is too little. They di'n't make any banging.'

Bagthorpe blood undeniably ran in Daisy's veins, and she did not give up. Casting around her for a suitable substitute for a drumstick, her eye fell upon a plate, knife and fork.

(Daisy had taken the sausages up, but had not been sufficiently conscientious as a waitress to return for the empties.) At Daisy's school there was a little percussion band. She had herself on occasion been allowed to strike a cymbal or shake a tambourine. The knife and fork suggested to her wholly acceptable percussion instruments. She had picked them up and hesitantly tapped them on the skins of the larger drums. An encouraging, if subdued, sound had resulted. Delighted, she had gradually increased the strength of her beat, and the drumming produced, although in no way to be compared with that achieved by the use of authentic drumsticks, was none the less gratifying.

Unfortunately, Daisy had a very low boredom threshold. If she had simply continued to keep up a subdued tattoo with her knife and fork until William's return, little or no damage would have been done. But the monotony of this exercise began to pall quite quickly.

In an attempt to increase the volume of noise produced by the drums, she had stuck the knife and fork, simultaneously, into the drum skins, as if tackling a steak and kidney pie. The result of this action, predictable as it would have been to an adult, had horrified Daisy only marginally less than William, who had at that moment returned, bearing his ill-gotten bacon and eggs.

Fact the Fifth

William, his eye falling straightway on the shocked Daisy, knife and fork in hand, and his shattered drums, had blown his mind.

'Something snapped in me,' he claimed. 'It would've snapped in anybody.'

'He *smacked* me!' cried Daisy. 'He smacked me hard on my bottom!'

'Hallelujah!' yelled Mr Bagthorpe. 'It's a breakthrough!'

'You beast!' squealed Rosie, and began to pummel William hard with her fists.

There was every sign that the furore would break out afresh when Mrs Bagthorpe, in ringing tones, commanded:

'Stop!'

They were so surprised that they stopped. Mrs Bagthorpe never raised her voice. She did not believe in it, and did deep breathing if ever she got tempted. Now her yoga had let her down.

'Is this true, William?' she demanded.

'Yes, it is,' he said. 'And if anybody'd ever smacked her before, my drums wouldn't have been shattered.'

'She needs smacking regularly,' Mr Bagthorpe said delightedly, 'to make up for lost time. We can only hope, William, that you have set a precedent.'

Daisy, at five, had never been smacked in her life. She had never even been shouted at, except by the Bagthorpes. All she had ever been was chided. Aunt Celia believed in letting Daisy have her way in all things, thinking thereby to encourage her freedom of expression. The walls of The Knoll, for instance, were thick with Daisy's crayoned thoughts and mottoes, and there were several little burned out corners where Daisy had lit fires during her Pyromaniac Phase.

'You had no business to smack Daisy, William,' Mrs Bagthorpe said. 'I am ashamed of you.'

'Violence breeds violence,' Grandma proclaimed. 'Daisy is a shining, innocent jewel of a child, and no finger should ever be raised against her.'

'Coming from you, Mother,' said Mr Bagthorpe, 'that is rich. When I was Daisy's age, you raised not only fingers against me, as I remember, but also walking-sticks and umbrellas. You are a whited sepulchre.'

'You were never innocent,' Grandma told him, unabashed. 'I would frequently despair of ever raising you as a recognizable human being at all. I am even now uncertain whether I succeeded.'

'But it's not fair!' Daisy now put her oar in again. 'William smacked me, and it *wasn't* me. It was Arry Awk!'

'Oh my God!' excaimed Mr Bagthorpe.

William, hollow-eyed and pale from shock and lack of sleep, looked as if again something was going to snap.

'Of course it was Arry Awk,' said Grandma calmly. 'I have never liked him, as you know, but I think I recognize his handiwork when I see it. Daisy is innocent.'

'And black,' gritted Mr Bagthorpe, 'is white! Arry Awk

is a member of Daisy's household, and Russell will foot the bill for those drums none the less.'

'And William will answer to him for striking an innocent and defenceless child,' replied Grandma. 'Come, Daisy. We must set about being immortal.'

'I don't sink I feel like living for ever today,' said Daisy dolefully.

'Nonsense!' Grandma said briskly. 'You are too sensitive, Daisy. You must learn not to let trivial matters upset you. Let us go and execute the first stage of our plan.'

'God help us all,' muttered Mr Bagthorpe, quite seriously, as the pair left the room. In the doorway they passed Tess, who had been unable to sleep for the noise of drumming, and had been copying Voltaire until 2 a.m. She too had black rings round her eyes and looked extremely ill-tempered.

Another row set up immediately, and only Jack appeared to notice that Daisy and Grandma were making extensive use of the telephone in the hall. By his reckoning, they made eight or nine calls. While recriminations were still flying, Mrs Fosdyke's key rattled noisily in the lock. Instant silence fell. The Bagthorpes had recently experienced the disruption produced in their lives by Mrs Fosdyke's absence, and had no wish to do so again. The row would have to be held in abeyance. They all sat and glared as Mrs Fosdyke scooted across the kitchen, whipping off her chiffon headscarf as she did so. She went to take a look at her uncompleted Portrait.

'Hmmm. Coming on all right, I s'pose,' she remarked. 'That frame'll make all the difference.'

The Bagthorpes were in no mood for fawning upon Mrs Fosdyke, but had to make the attempt.

'I think it's jolly good,' Jack offered. 'I think it's going to be the best Rosie's ever done.'

'She has, of course, an excellent subject,' said Mrs Bagthorpe, managing a smile of sorts.

' 'E's stopped that drumming, I see,' observed Mrs Fosdyke, setting up a rattle that was far louder than William's tattoo had ever been, even at close range. 'Well, thank the Lord for that. I try to stand things, but there's a limit. Got tired out, did 'e?'

'I was forced to give up because of a – because of a technical hitch,' William told her with dignity. 'Otherwise, I should have lasted for days – even weeks.'

'There's many as'd've give their notice years ago, of course. It's a marvel what I do put up with. Someone been frying again, has there? *Vitamings* is what I thought you wanted at Breakfast, Mrs Bagthorpe. There's plenty of 'em in grapefruit, and a great bowl of 'em here waiting to be ate. There's no vitamings in bacon and egg that I do know. Oranges and grape –'

'I am off to do some work,' Mr Bagthorpe announced. He could not stand Mrs Fosdyke at the best of times, and certainly could not sit and listen to her if she was going to start soliloquizing about vitamings.

'And I'm off to start a new scheme,' William said, following his father.

'What will that be, dear?' his mother asked timorously.

'I would rather not say, if you don't mind,' William told her. 'Some people are evidently not above sabotage, and it's safer.'

'Try to work in your rooms as much as possible today,' Mrs Bagthorpe told everybody. 'The decorators will be here, remember, and we want things to go as smoothly as possible.'

The Bagthorpes scattered, and the smooth day began.

Chapter 13

Mr Bagthorpe got his day off to a smooth start by telephoning The Knoll.

'I am afraid, Russell,' Jack heard him say with ill-concealed delight, 'that next time we see you we shall have another bill to present to you. Arry Awk has been at work again.'

There was a pause during which Jack presumed Uncle Parker was giving his opinion of Arry Awk, followed by a query as to the nature of his latest outrage.

'He has put a knife and fork through the skins of two very valuable drums,' Mr Bagthorpe told him. 'William expects the bill to be in the region of thirty pounds, and has asked me to intimate that an early settlement of the claim would be appreciated. These drums, which threaten the sanity of everyone else within earshot of them, appear to be vital to the sanity of their operator. It is my opinion, as you know, that in a previous incarnation he was a tribal warrior.'

Mr Bagthorpe threw in a few insults about Daisy for good measure, and retired to his study in high good humour.

The decorators then arrived. They inspected the two rooms, flung open all the windows in the sitting-room, and said they would start with the dining-room.

'Which is to be eau de nil,' Mrs Bagthorpe told them anxiously, 'whatever instructions you may receive to the contrary. If a small child with fair curls appears, would you be so good as to let me know immediately?'

They said they would. When his mother had gone Jack, who was sitting on the first landing listening to what went on below, heard the decorators discussing the house and its inmates. They made strong comment about the pungency of the sitting-room, and talked about whether they should demand an increased rate for going in there.

'Could ruin our lungs for life,' one said. 'Glad Fosdyke comes here, you know. Says the whole lot of 'em are mad as hatters. Especially him, she says. Says he's always standing on his head and shouting and setting fire to things.'

They set to work none the less. Upstairs Tess and William, Daisy and Grandma, were all presumably working on their projects for immortality behind closed doors. Jack, thinking that there was to be no further interesting action below, was about to fetch Zero and take him for a walk, when the telephone rang.

Mrs Fosdyke came scuttling out to answer it, but the call was for Mr Bagthorpe.

'I'll tell 'im,' she said, 'but 'e don't like being disturbed. Switches his own 'phone off, you know.'

She banged loudly on the study door.

'For you!' she shouted. 'It's the papers again.'

Jack flinched at this. He did not see how the Press could possibly have got wind of the drum episode, or that it would have been of interest as a news item. He felt certain, however, that if a newspaper was on the other end of the line, it boded ill for the Bagthorpes.

He was wrong. One of Mr Bagthorpe's dearest wishes was about to be fulfilled. He often, when in low spirits, talked about the way his work was passed over, and that of other, lesser writers, exalted. Whenever he read an article about any other television writer he would immediately embark on this theme at length, usually ending up by saying:

'I don't suppose Shakespeare ever got interviewed, either. There is not a shred of evidence that any article was ever written about him during his lifetime. Thank God I fall into the same category.'

He became particularly vociferous if a laudatory piece about another writer appeared in one of the Sunday heavies, from which his family deduced that one of his fiercest ambitions was to command a quarter page in the Review section of the *Sunday Times* (or failing that, the Colour Supplement).

This, quite exactly, was what was now being mooted. Jack had never seen his father so active on the telephone. He clutched at his hair, changed the receiver from one hand to the other, and paced up and down as far as the length of the flex would allow. Jack wondered if he had won the pools. (Mr Bagthorpe denied that he did the pools, but this did not mean anything.)

Mr Bagthorpe eventually came off the telephone (after a conversation of unprecedented politeness) and strode into the kitchen yelling:

'Laura! Quick! For God's sake! Quick!'

Jack himself hastily descended and found Mr Bagthorpe trying to convey to his wife the full impressiveness of the honour he was about to receive.

'The *Sunday Times*!' he yelled. 'Face to face interview with Gerald Pike! They're sending a photographer! My God! HENRY BAGTHORPE – HIS LIFE AND WORK! That'll show 'em! That'll show 'em who's taken seriously and who isn't. That'll put a few people's noses out of joint!'

(Mr Bagthorpe, having had his nose put considerably out

of joint so often in the past, was well qualified to judge this.)

'Lovely, darling!' cried Mrs Bagthorpe. 'But I thought you always said you didn't *want* to be interviewed.'

'Don't be a fool, Laura,' he told her. 'I was talking about all the phoney P.R. junk they usually do. This is a serious critical appraisal. This is in the Solzhenitsyn class.'

'Heavens!' His spouse could not but be impressed. 'When are they coming?'

'Tomorrow,' he told her. 'And I'm relying on you, Laura, to get an immediate grip on every member of this benighted household, and not loosen it till the whole thing's over. The first thing is to get that unholy infant and her hell-raising Arry Awk right out of here.'

'But we can hardly do that, Henry,' she protested. 'She only arrived yesterday.'

'And has already pulled in enough destruction to last most people a lifetime,' he returned. 'Where are they now? Where's Mother?'

'Mrs Bagthorpe Senior,' put in Mrs Fosdyke, 'come in here not half an hour ago and fetched a pile of them plastic carrier things out the cupboard. Not a plastic carrier left, I haven't got.'

'What for?' Mr Bagthorpe demanded.

'Not my business to ask,' replied Mrs Fosdyke, who had in fact asked, but had not been favoured with a reply. 'I hope I know better than to put my nose in where it ain't wanted.'

'They are not in the house, Henry,' Mrs Bagthorpe assured him. 'I saw them go myself. I'm sure you are alarming yourself unnecessarily. One would think, to hear you, that Mother and Daisy were perpetually out to make trouble. I'm sure they have gone on some quite harmless errand.'

'Then you are even more naïve than I took you to be,' he told her. 'Listen!'

They all heard the rush of gravel that invariably heralded the arrival of Uncle Parker. Mr Bagthorpe was pleased about this because he had something to boast of. He told Uncle Parker immediately of the forthcoming interview.

'Had to give it a bit of thought, of course,' he said, 'but agreed in the end. Fellow said I owed it to my public. And put like that, I could hardly refuse.'

'Indeed not,' Uncle Parker conceded. 'Congratulations, Henry. I hope everything will pass off without incident.'

'Why?' demanded Mr Bagthorpe, instantly suspicious. 'What made you say that? Why should it *not* pass off without incident?'

'Because, Henry,' replied Uncle Parker, 'this household does have a tendency to incident.'

'Particularly,' Mr Bagthorpe said, 'when that accursed daughter of yours is in the offing. Have you got that money for William?'

Uncle Parker fished for his wallet and Aunt Celia inquired:

'Is darling Daisy being made happy?'

Mrs Bagthorpe, the question being so phrased, was able to reply truthfully in the affirmative.

'We met her as we drove up,' Aunt Celia said dreamily. 'She and Mother – "crabbed age and youth". I almost wept to see them together in the sunshine.'

'I know the feeling,' Mr Bagthorpe told her. 'Sometimes I almost weep.'

'And how poetic, how symbolic, how *joyous*. . .'

Aunt Celia was somewhere off on her own. There were, however, key words in this enigmatic utterance that alerted Mr Bagthorpe.

'Poetic?' he repeated. 'Symbolic? Who?'

'Why, Daisy, of course,' she replied, 'and Mother whom she has taken by the hand. Ah, if but that all men could win immortality by so fair a means!'

'Look,' Mr Bagthorpe said, 'if that pair are up to something, I demand to know what.'

Aunt Celia's gaze rested momentarily and dreamily on Mr Bagthorpe's ireful countenance as it might on a stone or piece of bark. She did not read it.

'De la Mare,' she continued blissfully.

> 'I heard a little child beneath the stars
> Talk as he ran along
> To some sweet riddle in his mind that seemed
> A tip-toe into song.'

Mr Bagthorpe groaned.

'Any chance of your translating, Russell?' he asked.

Uncle Parker shook his head.

'Celia, Daisy and Mother share some secret,' he replied. 'Ours not to reason why.'

'Somebody's got to do some reasoning why around here,' said Mr Bagthorpe grimly. Then, to Celia, with extreme sarcasm:

'Did De la Mare, by the way, have anything to say about Arry Awk?'

He should have known better.

Aunt Celia, after a pensive pause, began:

> 'Someone is always sitting there
> In the little green orchard ...
> Even when –'

'Look!'

Mr Bagthorpe had by now had enough of Aunt Celia, whom he could only ever take in very small doses.

'If all Arry Awk ever did was to sit about in little green orchards, then this whole household would not now be in its present turmoil and you, Russell, would be hundreds of pounds better off. Get a grip on yourself, Celia.'

'I think actually, Henry, that will do,' observed Uncle Parker dangerously. He did not often drop his line of banter, but he was serious enough now. For some obscure reason he loved his wife to distraction. Jack could never understand it.

'You keep out of this,' Mr Bagthorpe told Uncle Parker. 'She's my sister, and I've known her longer than you have. She spent her entire childhood burbling about little green orchards and perilous seas and God knows what else. The only way Mother could ever get any sense out of her was by shaking her. Have *you* ever tried shaking her?'

He looked as if about to do this himself. Uncle Parker rose with an easy movement and interposed himself between them.

'That daughter of yours is going the same way!' Mr Bagthorpe was beginning to shout.

'If Daisy turns out exactly like Celia,' replied Uncle Parker fondly, 'then I ask for nothing more.'

At this confession of outright lunacy Mr Bagthorpe was stumped. The interval during which he was still shaking his head gave Mrs Bagthorpe an opportunity to pour oil on waters that were becoming more troubled by the moment.

'We are so proud of Henry,' she told the Parkers. 'At least, those of us who have heard. Perhaps you, Jack, could run up and tell Tess and William the news? And see where Father is?'

Jack executed this commission as quickly as he could because what he really wanted to do was set off with Zero on the track of Grandma and Daisy. He found Tess painstakingly reversing Voltaire to manuscript form and clearly becoming very tired of this.

'He's so *verbose*,' she told Jack. 'Long-winded. If his style was any good, his books would be half the length they are.'

'I should pack it in,' Jack advised. 'I don't honestly think it's worth it.'

'What's William doing?' she demanded.

'I'm just off to see,' he told her. 'Don't forget to say jolly good to Father when you see him.'

She made no answer to this, and Jack went along to see whether Grandpa was in his room. He was, watching Playschool on a portable television.

'First class stuff, this,' he greeted Jack. 'Never had it when *I* was young.'

Jack supposed this was why Grandpa was so keen on it now. He was making up for lost time – or in his second childhood, which Jack knew to be a possibility. He shouted out the news of Mr Bagthorpe's achievement, and Grandpa nodded encouragingly.

'Good paper, *The Times*,' he said. 'Wish we could still afford it. Henry'll enjoy seeing one of his plays in there. Never used to print plays, in the old days, but times change, of course, I know that.'

Jack gleaned from this that Grandpa's hearing aid was in one of its bad patches – which meant that it was very likely to rain later. Grandpa's hearing aid was often consulted for weather forecasts. He left Grandpa thinking that the *Sunday Times* was to publish one of Mr Bagthorpe's plays, and went on to William.

As he mounted the second flight Jack could hear the crackles and bleeps that meant William had his headphones on. Jack could guess whom he was trying to contact. Grandma, when she felt low or threatened, talked to Thomas, Daisy, apparently, to Arry Awk. William talked to Anonymous from Grimsby.

When Jack entered William made such furious dismissive gestures that Jack fished for a pen, wrote 'Father is going to be in the *Sunday Times*' on a torn-out page from his diary, and placed it near William. He caught sight of the drums before he left. Daisy had certainly tucked well into them with her knife and fork.

When Jack went back downstairs, Zero at his heels, the Parkers had left, and Mr Bagthorpe had presumably gone back into his study to think of intelligent and enigmatic things to say the following day. Mrs Bagthorpe, lulled into a temporary sense of security by the knowledge that Grandma and Daisy were not in the house, was about to mount to her room and sort out her Problems.

'Me and Zero are just off for a walk and a bit of tracking practice,' Jack told her.

As they set off down the garden toward the meadow Jack, casting his eyes upward, reflected that Grandpa's hearing aid had come up trumps again.

'We'll have to look sharp, old chap,' he told Zero. 'Going to rain buckets.'

They padded along companionably while Jack kept up a running pep talk, as he often did when they were alone, to keep Zero's ears and spirits up.

'You'll probably be in the *Sunday Times* as well, old chap,' he told Zero. 'Not that it matters to you. You're immortal anyway.'

Jack encountered Grandma and Daisy in the village looking uncommonly pleased with themselves. Each was carrying two plastic bags filled with something or other. Jack could not make out what, but had the impression that whatever it was was soft and light.

'What've you got there?' he asked them.

'Soon you will know all,' Grandma replied aggravatingly. Jack did not for a moment believe that what the plastic carriers held was Top Secret. It was just that Grandma liked secrecy. When Jack realized he was going to get nothing out of either of them he decided to branch off on his own to return across the meadow, though not without first imparting Mr Bagthorpe's news.

'I shouldn't let him see those bags,' he warned. 'He's already in a bit of a lather.'

'The day I become frightened of my own son will be the Day of Judgement,' Grandma told him. 'I care not a fig for Henry. When did you say this interview was to take place?'

'Tomorrow.'

'And a photographer, you said?'

'Yes.'

Jack saw an unmistakable look pass over Grandma's face.

It was a look that all members of the Bagthorpes ménage knew, and one they preferred not to see appear. It was a compound of excitement and pleasure, tinged with malice. It was also the harbinger of doom. It was, Jack thought, the equivalent of dead men rising and owls screeching at noon in Shakespeare's plays. (He was not familiar with the Collected Works, nor even very familiar with *Julius Caesar*.)

'Father had better look out, old chap,' he told Zero after parting company with the Unholy Alliance. 'Perhaps we'd all better. When we get back, I'm going to look up Armageddon in the dictionary. I think it might be coming.'

Chapter 14

What Grandma and Daisy had been doing all morning was picking daisies in a field the other side of the village. They had begun to collect their daisies there because it was well away from Unicorn House, and Grandma wished to keep this activity secret for as long as possible. The scheme had been hatched up the previous day, and was Grandma's brain-child.

'We shall probably need a million daisies,' she had told a wide-eyed Daisy.

'But we can't pick a million daisies, Grandma Bag,' Daisy objected. 'We're too old and too young.'

'We shall delegate,' Grandma said. 'Have you any friends?'

'Not exackly friends,' Daisy admitted, 'excepting Arry Awk.'

'Arry Awk will be left strictly out of this enterprise, Daisy,' Grandma told her. 'Is that clearly understood?'

'Yes, Grandma Bag,' said Daisy meekly.

'I don't suppose he has ever picked daisies in his life,' Grandma went on, 'and would certainly not know how to make a chain.'

What Grandma and Daisy were going to do was make the longest daisy chain in the world. This would ensure their joint immortality in the shape of an entry in the *Guinness Book of Records*, Grandma said.

'And what is more,' she added, 'it is a very beautiful,

poetic and symbolic gesture. Even Celia would admit that.'

'Why is it, Grandma Bag?' inquired Daisy.

'Because, dear child, your *name* is Daisy,' Grandma told her, 'and because a daisy chain is an intrinsically poetic thing. More poems have been written in the English language about daisy chains than any other subject. Now, what about these friends of yours? We shall not be able to pick a million daisies single-handed.'

Daisy supplied the names of several small girls in the village who she thought might help, particularly as Grandma intended to offer them an inducement. That morning she had telephoned nine or ten of them, promising a signed poster of Zero for each plastic carrier full of daisies.

'Though the stems must be long,' she warned. 'I do not want bags full of daisy heads with half-inch stems. No stems, no poster. And this is a secret. If you tell – no poster.'

Jack, of course, as yet knew nothing of this. As he approached the stile on the outskirts of the village, the first heavy drops of rain began to fall. He hurried his step, and was amazed to see what at first sight looked like a horde, but was probably around a dozen, small girls squealing and running pell mell towards him, carrying plastic carriers.

This had a very odd effect on Jack. He had just seen Daisy and Grandma with their carriers. He knew that they were set on some deadly enterprise. And now here was an army they seemed to have enlisted. Their rings were widening ominously beyond their immediate family into the outside world.

The implications were frightening. Jack stood and let the little girls stream past him over the stile, squealing and giggling, their hair already soaked. He stood aside, not out of politeness, but in the hope that one of the fugitives might fall, and tip out the contents of her carrier. He was even tempted to give one of them a push.

When they were all gone Jack and Zero themselves set off at a run over the wet grass, while the squeals of the Unholy Alliance's mercenaries faded into the distance.

Grandma and Daisy arrived home some twenty minutes later than Jack, themselves considerably wet. They went cheerfully upstairs to change into dry things, and Jack noted that they did not have their carriers.

'Perhaps,' he thought with relief, 'whatever they're going to do, they're not going to do it here.'

He was mistaken in this assumption. They were going to do it there, but in view of the news given them by Jack, Grandma proposed to change the timing of the enterprise.

'We shall do it tomorrow,' she told Daisy. 'This rain is exactly what we need, to keep the daisies fresh. We will secrete them in the shrubbery for the time being.'

The plastic sacks, then, were at the present time concealed among some laurels in the drive, to have their contents properly spread out later.

Daisy and Grandma reappeared just as lunch was being served, bright-eyed and their hair still hanging in damp ringlets. Mr Bagthorpe eyed them keenly.

'Where have you been?' he demanded.

'Out in the rain, Henry dear,' Grandma replied, 'as I should have thought was apparent.'

'You know perfectly well what I mean,' he told her. 'You know perfectly well that you and Daisy are about to make a concerted pitch for immortality. And I want an assurance from you now, at this moment, that you will not do it tomorrow, in this house. If such an assurance is not forthcoming, Daisy departs forthwith.'

'Tomorrow is rather an important day for Henry, you see, dear,' Mrs Bagthorpe told Grandma. 'He is to be interviewed and photographed by the *Sunday Times*.'

'So I understand,' replied Grandma, 'and I congratulate him. Daisy and I will not make our attempt tomorrow, in this house.'

This carefully worded assurance seemed to satisfy Mr Bagthorpe (though he should have been alerted by the readiness with which it was given) because he had not considered the possibility that the attempt would be made tomorrow, in the garden. Daisy and Grandma exchanged smiles that only Jack seemed to observe.

After lunch Mr Bagthorpe proposed to drive the family into Aysham to change library books and so on. He could not, he told them, sit still in his study, because of nervous agitation.

'It is part of the heavy price of genius,' he said.

Most of the family opted to go with him, but Jack announced his intention of remaining behind. He felt this to be his duty. Grandma and Daisy in their present volatile state needed constant supervision. Unfortunately, his mother insisted that he go. His hair needed cutting, she said, and so did William's.

'You may have your photographs taken tomorrow,' she told them, 'and I wish to feel proud of you.'

Mr Bagthorpe endorsed this, saying that while he fervently hoped the *Sunday Times* would not photograph them, or indeed any other members of the family, if by any chance they did he, Mr Bagthorpe, did not wish to appear as having fathered so hirsute a tribe.

Jack nearly told his parents his reason for wanting to remain behind, but felt confused as to where his loyalties lay. He had no real wish to sabotage Daisy and Grandma, who at any rate did not shout at Zero and constantly undermine him, as Mr Bagthorpe did. He decided to keep his mouth shut and let things take their natural course.

When the Bagthorpes arrived back at tea-time things had taken a considerable course. As they entered the drive, Jack thought he caught a glimpse of one of the decorators up a tree. This seemed so unlikely an eventuality that he did not, at the time, mention it. The front door was ajar, so there was evidently someone about, though it did not feel as if there were. The house had an abandoned air that was at first hard to pinpoint, and then –

'The decorators!' exclaimed Mrs Bagthorpe. 'They are not supposed to leave until half-past five!'

She ran to the dining-room and flung open the door, and saw to her relief that all tins of paint were tightly closed, according to her instructions, and that the walls were not toad colour, as she had half expected, but still eau de nil.

'Mother!' she called, returning to the hall. 'Daisy!'

There was no reply. At this point Jack decided to mention the decorator up the tree.

'*What?*' Mr Bagthorpe, who had been about to enter the study, whirled about and went straight back through the front door.

'Mother!' he yelled. 'Daisy!'

William with an attempt at facetiousness, cupped his hands together and bawled:

'Arry Awk!'

Mr Bagthorpe bounded through the shrubbery, followed by the rest. There on the lawn beyond were Grandma and Daisy and one of the decorators. The other, Jack perceived, *was* up a tree.

'What in the name of heaven is going on?' demanded Mr Bagthorpe.

'Moderate your voice please, Henry,' Grandma replied. 'I am not deaf, and Daisy is of a sensitive disposition. These gentlemen are very kindly putting up my floodlights for me.'

'Are very kindly *what*?' repeated Mr Bagthorpe.

He looked wildly about him and saw lengths of cable looped from tree to tree and lying in coils. He also spotted the decorator who was up the tree. He was struggling to lash a floodlight to a low branch.

'Shan't be a minute, sir!' the decorator shouted. 'Nearly finished.'

'Oh dear!' said Mrs Bagthorpe faintly.

When the decorator climbed down, Mr Bagthorpe was very rude to him.

'I was give my instructions by Mrs Bagthorpe Senior,' said the decorator stiffly. 'And I obeyed them.'

'You are being paid to paint walls, not loop lights round in trees,' gritted Mr Bagthorpe.

'We are aware of that,' the decorator told him. 'Was you expecting your mother to go climbing trees at her age?'

'She can climb whatever she likes,' returned Mr Bagthorpe.

'The only hinstruction I received,' said the second decorator, 'was to inform your good lady if I was to see a small child with curls. That child is here, madam, as you will hobserve, and am duly reporting it.'

'Thank you, Mr Swann,' said Mrs Bagthorpe weakly.

'Reporting it!' yelled Mr Bagthorpe. 'We can *see* she's here, for God's sake. And where are these lights from? What're they for?'

'They are from the vicar, Henry,' Grandma told him. 'Thank you so much, gentlemen. I am most grateful.'

She opened her purse and gave two pound notes to the foreman under Mr Bagthorpe's furious glare. The decorators ambled off back to the house and Mr Bagthorpe turned his attention to the Unholy Alliance.

'Mother,' he began, 'what, in the name of all that is wonderful – is – going – on?'

'There's no need to space your words out at me like that, Henry,' Grandma told him. 'I am not interfering with your life. Pray do not interfere with mine.'

'Grandma Bag and me's going to make the longest daisy chain in the whole world, Uncle Bag,' Daisy then piped up. 'We'll be in the Beginners' Book of Records.'

Jack at once saw the light.

'You – are – what?'

'I think you heard, Henry,' said Grandma. 'And you are still spacing out your words.'

'Will you help, Uncle Bag?' asked Daisy.

This optimistic request met with a sound more like an animal growl than a human rejoinder, and Mr Bagthorpe turned on his heel and lurched back towards the house, holding his head in his hands.

'Oh dear,' said Mrs Bagthorpe, 'Mother, is this true?'

'Perfectly true, Laura,' replied Grandma, 'and I am astonished that there should be all this ridiculous fuss. I should have thought that making a daisy chain was the most harmless occupation in the world. I should have thought that even Henry could not have taken exception to it. One really begins to wonder if one can ever do anything right.'

'We had better go and have a cup of tea,' said Mrs Bagthorpe weakly at length. 'Whatever have floodlights to do with daisy chains?'

This point was clarified over tea in the kitchen, when Grandma outlined her scheme to an interested audience which did not include Mr Bagthorpe. Grandma was a schemer of the first order. If she had a project in hand, she executed it with the ruthless efficiency of a military genius. The present case was no exception.

The reason for the floodlights, she explained, was that darkness might fall the following day before the daisy chain was long enough. She had telephoned the vicar and asked for the loan of the floodlights that had been used for the *son et lumière* performance in the vicarage garden by the Ladies' Fellowship. In this, Grandma had played the part of Queen Elizabeth I and had, according to Mr Bagthorpe, been playing it ever since.

'If necessary, Daisy and I will work through till dawn breaks the following day,' Grandma informed them all.

No one had reason to doubt this.

'It would be a pity, however,' she continued, 'for an elderly lady and a delicate child to have to sit out all night in a heavy dew.'

'It would be madness, Mother,' agreed Mrs Bagthorpe instantly, visualizing Aunt Celia's reaction to this proposal. 'I think you must forget all about it.'

'Also,' continued Grandma, ignoring her, 'there has been an unfortunate development during the afternoon. We wish, as I have told you, to establish a record for the longest daisy chain in the world. I believed this to be an entirely original enterprise. However, I find that I am mistaken. One of Daisy's friends has told us that a record for this already exists.'

'And there aren't enough of us,' Daisy chipped in. 'We've got enough daisies, we've got bags and bags of daisies, but we haven't got enough of us.'

The Bagthorpes waited for this obscure utterance to be clarified.

'What Daisy is saying,' Grandma told them obligingly, 'is that we shall have to enlist your help. Fetch me that book, Daisy.'

Daisy trotted out and soon reappeared carrying the *Guinness Book of Records*, which was beginning to look very thumbed around the edges, having been gone through many times with a fine toothcomb by Bagthorpes bent on immortality.

'I will read the appropriate entry,' Grandma told them. Accordingly she read: ' "The longest daisy chain on record is one of 3,234 ft, 985 m, made of 18,000 daisies by the members of the Deanery Players, Harrogate, North Yorkshire, England, in 8½ hours on 12th July 1975." '

'Crikey!' Rosie exclaimed. 'Three thousand and *how* many feet?'

'I don't think you'll manage it, Grandma,' Jack told her.

'Precisely,' she nodded. 'The chain, you will note, was not made singlehanded by an elderly lady and a delicate child. It was made by some people called the Deanery Players. I do not know who these people are, or how many of them there were, but I should imagine they were in rude health, and numbered more than two.'

'There's only two of us, you see,' Daisy elaborated helpfully.

'Daisy and I could, of course, make the attempt to establish a record for the longest chain made by a five-year-old child and her grandmother,' Grandma said.

'But if we *all* helped,' cried Rosie, 'we'd all be in! Instead of those Player people, it would say "the Bagthorpes". It might even give all our names separately. That'd show that Esther.'

'That is exactly the point,' Grandma nodded. 'I am willing to share with you all my chance of immortality.'

There was a pause, while people thought about this offer. There seemed, particularly to Tess and William, something intrinsically frivolous and undeserving of serious acclaim about the making of a daisy chain, however long. It was not at all what they had had in mind. On the other hand, Esther and Luke were unlikely, whatever their current success, to achieve the kind of kudos that goes with being an entry in the *Guinness Book of Records*. William, even when his drums were mended, had no intention of starting his endurance test again, because he had in fact already had quite enough of it by the time Daisy came on the scene with her knife and fork (though he would not admit this). Tess, suffering horribly from writer's cramp, and even wondering if her eyesight were beginning to fail, saw in the daisy chain a loophole, as it were, for escape without loss of face.

'I'll help,' Rosie said.

'And me,' Jack said.

'It will mean my sacrificing my own immortality,' Tess said ponderingly, 'but, of course, family honour must come first. Very well, Grandma, I shall give you my assistance.'

'Thank you, Tess,' said Grandma, and looked inquiringly at William. He was well aware that sixteen-year-old males do not normally make daisy chains, but was unwilling to miss out on the immortality stakes.

'All right,' he said at length. 'But I'm not doing any of the picking.'

'There will be no need,' Grandma told him. 'The picking has already been done. I should imagine that we already have at least 18,000 daisies. But there are further supplies in at least two fields that Daisy and I know of, and if we require them, we shall send for them.'

'They've got lots of little girls picking for them,' Jack told him. 'I saw them this morning. They had bags full.'

'I wonder how many of those Deanery people there were,' William said. 'Three thousand whatever it was feet sounds an awful lot. Can we beat them, do you think?'

'Of course we can,' Grandma returned calmly. 'We can beat anybody.'

'I will certainly lend a hand during the odd moment,' Mrs Bagthorpe volunteered, not wishing to appear discouraging towards any efforts on the part of her offspring to extend themselves. (Though she did not consider that daisy chain making constituted an Extra String to anybody's Bow.)

'You will not be allowed to,' Grandma told her.

Mrs Bagthorpe looked startled by this outright rejection of her services.

'You are not a Blood Bagthorpe, Laura,' Grandma explained. 'You are related only by marriage, and not strictly one of the family. We do not wish to risk being disqualified on a technical point.'

'Oh!' Mrs Bagthorpe was quite nonplussed. She could see that Grandma's ruling would qualify Aunt Celia and Mr Bagthorpe, but hoped that Grandma would have the wisdom not to invite the latter. Grandma went on to say that she had explained the matter to Grandpa, and he would be happy to help.

'Just a minute,' William said. 'If Mother's not a true Bagthorpe, nor are you. *You only* married one.'

Grandma drew herself up exceedingly at this heresy.

'I am the head of the line,' she stated. 'You are all descended from me. I hope you are not going to deny that?'

No one did, though they all thought her logic shaky.

'I shall telephone Celia,' she went on, 'and enlist her aid. She is, of course, hopeless at most things, but daisy chains might turn out to be one of her strengths.'

Aunt Celia was, indeed, ecstatic about the venture, and said what poetry Daisy had in her soul to think of something like this, appearing not to hear Grandma's frequently repeated assertions that it was *she* who had had the idea. Aunt Celia also saw the project as symbolic.

'I shall write a poem about it,' she promised.

Once the Bagthorpes had thrown in their lot with Grandma, they became wholly involved in it. Jack, who thought the little girls he had seen in the meadow had looked rather silly and unreliable, volunteered to go down and check on their bags of daisies.

'Tell them to lay them on sheets of polythene,' Grandma instructed, 'and water them frequently with a fine rose.'

Rosie offered to take Daisy on a further picking expedition, because she was afraid they might run out of daisies. William said that he would set his alarm clock for 2 a.m., and go down and check on their daisies and water them further if necessary. He then went out to ensure that the floodlights were working. Tess had pointed out that the Deanery Players had made their chain in only eight and a half hours and had had no need of floodlights. William told her that a mathematical equation would be involved, and spelled it out to her.

'It is a question of persons, per number of daisies per hour,' he said.

Grandma said that she did not care if there had been a hundred Deanery Players. The Bagthorpes would beat all comers, she proclaimed, and this, in fact, was by now the general feeling.

The only member of the household not obsessively involved in the Great Bagthorpe Daisy Chain was Mr Bagthorpe himself. He accused Grandma of plotting the whole thing in order to ruin his reputation.

'I shall telephone the *Sunday Times* and tell them not to come,' he said.

He did not, of course, do this. He could not feel sufficiently confident that they would then arrange an alternative date.

'I may well sit up all night,' he stated. 'I shall not be able to close my eyes. Any chance of my ever being taken seriously as a writer has now gone, knocked from my grasp by my own family.'

'If you do,' William said, 'it would save me setting the alarm. Could you go out from time to time and see if the daisies need watering, do you think?'

Chapter 15

Next day the Bagthorpes were up at dawn, raring to go. They had a hasty and noisy breakfast – with the exception of Mr Bagthorpe, who was still fast asleep. William collected all the waterproofs in the house, because there had been a very heavy dew, and everyone except Grandma and Grandpa would be sitting on the ground.

With enormous anticipation they then set out into the unaccustomed stillness of early morning. The birds were whistling, and a milky haze hung in the distance.

'It feels like going on holiday,' Jack said. 'Come on, Zero old chap. You're going to guard.'

'My fingers feel all shaky,' Rosie confided in them all. 'I'm so excited, I don't know if I'll be able to use them properly.'

'Then you must pull yourself together,' Grandma told her. 'Daisies are a precious commodity. We do not want any unnecessary wastage.'

The daisies were pulled out and spread in the middle of the lawn. There seemed acres of them, lying thickly in the kind of quantities nobody had ever seen before. Their appearance produced a temporary, awed silence.

'We are embarking on a task of Herculean proportions,' Tess remarked at last. 'Personally, I would rather tackle the Augean stables.'

'We want none of that kind of defeatist talk!' Grandma snapped. 'Where's your spirit?'

They all arranged themselves round, and Grandma picked up a handful of daisies and placed them in her lap.

'I shall now thread the first two daisies,' she announced, making this moment into a kind of grand opening ceremony. 'Daisy will then thread the next. The rest of you can start in whatever order you like.'

They watched as she carefully nipped the stem of one daisy, and passed through the slit the stem of another. She then looked triumphantly about her, as if expecting a round of applause. None was forthcoming.

'It is fortunate that none of us bite our nails,' Grandma observed – and it was, of course. (Jack used to, but gave it up after Zero became famous.)

After that, they all began. They worked fast, and in almost total silence, because they were as yet overcome by the enormity of what they were attempting.

They had been working for well over an hour, and getting to the point where they were having to spread further apart, to avoid tangling their chains, when Mrs Fosdyke arrived. She came up the drive at a brisk hedgehog trot and they heard her footsteps though they could not see her.

'Here, Mrs Fosdyke!' called Mrs Bagthorpe. (She was not being allowed to thread, but Grandma had said she could keep everybody else supplied with daisies.) She realized afterward that she should have got up, joined Mrs Fosdyke, and explained slowly and carefully what was taking place, to break it to her gently.

As it was, next moment Mrs Fosdyke's head poked through a shrub, disembodied like the Cheshire Cat's, but unlike that cat, not smiling. Her expression was one of horror and downright disbelief. She blinked her eyes rapidly, evidently not trusting them.

'Oh my good gracious!' she exclaimed at last. 'Now what?'

'We are making the longest daisy chain in the world, Mrs

Fosdyke!' Grandma called gaily. She had by now worked into a kind of rhythm with her daisies, and her hands were moving with a regular action as though she were crocheting, or knitting. She gave the impression that now she had started, she was never going to stop.

'I don't believe it!' Mrs Fosdyke said flatly. She pushed right past the shrub and stood there clutching her black plastic carrier, staring about her. 'I don't believe it!' she repeated, as if by so doing she could make the whole scene disappear.

It seemed to Mrs Fosdyke, who had been the witness of innumerable Bagthorpian débâcles, that the peaceful, innocent tableau that now lay before her was the most unnerving sight of her career with them. It was still not yet eight o'clock, and they sat steadily and patiently threading as if they might have been there all night – or even from time immemorial. If Mrs Fosdyke had ever read Kafka, or had known about surrealism, she would have recognized the disturbing quality they invoked. But she had not, and could only struggle to find the right words to describe how she had felt later, in The Fiddler's Arms.

'You don't expect a turn like that, eight o'clock in the morning,' she told her interested audience. 'It ain't in nature. Young and old alike, sitting like statchers, putting daisies together as if they was Snow White. If I was ten years older I should have dropped dead at my own feet.'

At the time, she simply stood rooted to the spot, trying to order her thoughts.

'We have breakfasted already,' Grandma told her, 'but I am sure we would all appreciate a cup of tea, when you have a moment.'

'Cup of tea,' Mrs Fosdyke repeated mechanically. 'Cup of tea.'

She disappeared among the foliage, away toward the sanity of her kitchen, the kettle and the teapot. Jack was excused for several minutes, to go and help her carry the trays of tea. He found her tracking about the kitchen and talking to herself.

'I've come to help carry,' he told her, in a fairly loud voice, to be sure of getting through to her. She stopped and stared at him.

'They're sitting out there making daisy chains,' she told him, as if hoping to be contradicted. 'I saw them. I saw them with my own eyes.'

'That's right,' he agreed. 'I know it seems a bit funny, but –'

'Ought I to telephone somebody?' she wondered aloud.

At this point Mr Bagthorpe entered.

'Where are they?' he demanded.

'On the front lawn,' Jack told him.

'Making daisy chains?'

'Yes. Well, we did tell you we were.'

Mrs Fosdyke was astonished to see Mr Bagthorpe. She assumed that he, as the maddest of the lot, had been among the chain-makers – that he was, in fact, their organizer. If all the Bagthorpes had gone mad *except* him, then the plot, so far as she was concerned, was thickening.

'The *Sunday Times* will approach my house, and will find my entire family, including my own mother, up to their ears in daisies,' said Mr Bagthorpe, summing up the situation for himself. 'Nothing like this can ever have happened to a serious writer before. Would Shakespeare have survived, I wonder, or Tolstoy, or Milton, if any of their families were on record as having been discovered like this? Could we now take *Othello* seriously, or *Paradise Lost*, if this were so?'

'I suppose you couldn't pretend we *weren't* your family,' Jack suggested helpfully.

Mr Bagthorpe turned on him a weary gaze.

'So the situation improves,' he said. 'I have a bunch of complete strangers in my garden looping miles of daisy chain around, and I pass it off. I say, "Sorry the family aren't here to meet you – just ignore that bunch of lunatics on the front lawn. It happens every day in the daisy season." '

'I suppose not,' Jack admitted.

A loud rush of gravel was heard in the ensuing silence.

'That,' said Mr Bagthorpe, 'is all I need.'

Uncle Parker had arrived to bring his wife to the daisy-chaining. He was himself debarred from taking part because of Grandma's ruling about blood.

'No reason why *you* shouldn't lend a hand, though, Henry,' he told Mr Bagthorpe, appropriating two of Mrs Fosdyke's cups of tea for himself and Aunt Celia. 'What a scoop for the Colour Supplement this will be.'

'If it were not for your accursed daughter,' Mr Bagthorpe told him, 'none of this would have happened.'

'That is the truth!' cried Aunt Celia surprisingly. 'And we are proud to own it! Such poetry, such symbolism – and only five years of age!'

There was a moment's silence while everyone else present thought their own thoughts about Daisy.

'Better get out there and see how they're doing,' Uncle Parker said. 'And get Celia started. Sure you won't come, Henry?'

Aunt Celia, with cooing and exclamations of bliss, took her place among the daisy-threaders. Jack and Mrs Fosdyke darted among them passing cups of tea.

'Delicious!' remarked Grandma, pausing to take a sip. 'I

always think tea tastes so much better when one is making daisy chains.'

The morning wore on and the chains lengthened by the minute. By lunch-time the Bagthorpe lawn looked like a miniature maze with a lot of people lost in it. William, feeling this to be a marginally more manly role, had appointed himself overseer and measurer. Being Bagthorpes, they had been unable to resist setting up a race within a race, and were vying with one another to produce the longest individual chain. At present it looked as if Tess would win, or Grandma. Aunt Celia was very nimble with her fingers, but lost much time going into reveries, during which she would sit with her hands folded in her lap, dreamily gazing about her and presumably drinking in all the poetry and symbolism.

It was stew for lunch, as luck would have it, and Grandma did not say anything about this tasting so much better when eaten in conjunction with daisy chains.

'I should have thought cucumber sandwiches would have been more apt,' she told Mrs Fosdyke, 'followed by raspberries and cream.'

'There's bakewell tart and custard to follow,' Mrs Fosdyke told her.

It was unfortunate that a photographer from the *Aysham Gazette* arrived during the working up of mouthfuls of stew between daisy-threading, because the resulting picture was anything but poetic and symbolic. The photographer came and went without Mr Bagthorpe's knowledge, and had been invited, of course, by Grandma. Mr Bagthorpe was exaggerating only a little when he said, as he often did, that Grandma had become drunk with the heady wine of publicity.

By two o'clock the Bagthorpes had been working for six and a half hours, and tension was running high. William had told them that their individual quota of daisies to be threaded was to be in the region of four and a half thousand each, if the existing record were to be broken.

'Though if we beat it by only one daisy,' he added, 'it will still constitute an authentic record.'

If the time-record were to be broken too, the Great Bagthorpe Daisy Chain was due to be completed by 3.22 p.m. William, dizzied by his task of looping and numbering daisies by the yard, and by the complexity of the calculations to be made, panicked, and rang for three of his friends to come and assist. William himself counted Grandma's chain and made it three thousand seven hundred and one. He calculated rapidly, and realized that if this were accurate, and roughly matched by the rest, the record was as good as in the bag. This announcement caused so much excitement and jubilation that William began to wonder if he had perhaps made an error, and started a recount.

At just before half-past two, Jack said, 'I think it's going to rain again.'

Grandma looked up.

'Alfred,' she called loudly to Grandpa. 'Alfred.'

He carried on picking at his daisies with his short, blunt fingers.

'Go and fetch all the umbrellas in the house,' she ordered Jack. 'Fetch the two large garden umbrellas from the shed.'

He did so. As he returned with them the first heavy drops of rain were splashing down.

'The rain will help to keep the daisies fresh,' Grandma observed.

She was enthroned under one of the striped sun umbrellas,

with Grandpa, as her consort, occupying a marginal position on the other side of the handle. The other Bagthorpes fended for themselves as best they could, retiring under trees, and wedging umbrellas above themselves in the boughs.

'Isn't it *lovely*!' squealed Daisy, crouched under her umbrella like a gnome under a deadly toadstool. 'Rain, rain, bootiful rain, bootiful pea-green rain. . .'

William's three friends arrived and, once they had recovered from the shock of what they saw, set about checking William's reckonings. Conversation among the daisy-chainers themselves was now banned.

'No one must speak,' William told them, 'including you, Grandma. If we are distracted, and lose count, we are lost.'

What the men from the *Sunday Times* found, then, when they arrived at Unicorn House at around three, was what looked at first sight like a heavy local fall of snow being sat in by a large number of people. And what they heard, when they stepped out of the car and gingerly approached, was the low murmur of people counting.

'Seven ninety-six, seven ninety-seven, seven ninety-eight. . .'

Running beneath this, like a counterpoint, was a soft refrain.

'Rain, rain, bootiful rain, bootiful pea-green rain. . .'

The *Sunday Times* men stood baffled, taking in this bizarre scene. They had heard rumours about Mr Bagthorpe's unpredictability. Some people had even used the word 'unbalanced'. Was this, they wondered, an elaborate tableau staged for their benefit? Was its perpetrator, perhaps, concealed nearby, watching to see its effect? They shook their heads in unison. Both these men had been all over the world, and were not easily impressed by anything, but they were impressed by this.

'What,' muttered one to the other under his breath, 'in the name of God is going on, do you think?'

The photographer took another long look.

'They're making daisy chains, I think,' he pronounced.

At this point Mr Bagthorpe, carefully dressed with careless negligence, emerged. He at once started in on an apology for his family, making strenuous denials of any involvement with their present activities. His voice got louder until he was finally yelling.

'Be quiet!' called Grandma from under her canopy. 'We shall lose count.'

The photographer was already making adjustments to his camera.

'Switch on the floodlights!' came Grandma's voice. 'This poor light is trying to my eyes.'

The photographer became almost hysterical when the powerful floodlights suddenly bathed his subjects under their umbrellas.

'Floodlights!' he gibbered. 'My God – it's too good to be true. I've even got them *lit*!'

Then he was in among them, crouching and leaping, his shutter clicking non-stop. Gerald Pike started to try to interview the daisy-chainers, but was severely rebuked by Grandma, who was not so impressed by the *Sunday Times* as her son was.

'This morbid prying into personal lives must stop,' she told him. 'When we have made the longest daisy chain in the world, then I will interview you.'

Mr Bagthorpe, gritting his teeth, started to stroll among the workers, hoping that Gerald Pike would remember his original intention of interviewing *him*.

'Oh, go *'way*, Uncle Bag!' Daisy squealed as he tripped over her thread and snapped it.

Gerald Pike did then turn his attention to Mr Bagthorpe.

'Which chain is yours?' he inquired.

'I don't have a chain,' Mr Bagthorpe told him. 'I am a serious creative –'

'But I understood this was a family effort. The Great Bagthorpe Daisy Chain. Perhaps you feel it is beneath you?' (Gerald Pike was sufficiently seasoned a journalist to recognize that the story as it stood was good, but with Mr Bagthorpe also deeply involved, would be better.)

'Perhaps you feel it is beneath you?' he repeated, seeing that Mr Bagthorpe was trying to restrain himself.

'Perhaps I do!' shouted Mr Bagthorpe, rising to this. 'Perhaps I think the whole mutton-headed, half-baked...'

He stopped. Gerald Pike was making notes. Mr Bagthorpe looked wildly about him. It was like a nightmare. His whole family was sitting in the rain under umbrellas and lit eerily by floodlights, patiently threading daisies. He was evidently now expected to join them. His wife appeared at his elbow.

'Look, Henry dear,' she said, 'this is how you do it.'

At this point a distraction occurred in the shape of Tess accusing Grandma of appropriating several yards of her daisies. The two had been running almost neck and neck for the individual title, and now, all of a sudden, Grandma was unassailably in the lead.

'You took some of my chain while I was fixing my umbrella!' Tess cried.

'Tess, dear,' said Grandma piously, 'the day I am reduced to cheating will be the day I retire from all forms of competitive activity.'

This shameless denial left everybody speechless. Grandma

always cheated, at everything, and the Bagthorpes knew it. If on this occasion she had *not* cheated, then this would in itself constitute a record. Matters were taking a dangerous turn, with Tess threatening to snap off the end of Grandma's chain in retaliation, when William, who had been in consultation with his aides, shouted:

'That's it! We've done it!'

A concerted cheer set up from the Bagthorpes. They stood up and let the rain pour down on them, and cheered themselves hoarse. They all began boasting at once.

'We're in the *Guinness Book of Records*!' shouted Rosie.

'Hurray hurray aren't we clever!' squealed Daisy. 'And Arry Awk! He did half my chain!'

'William, kindly go and ask Mrs Fosdyke to fetch out the champagne I laid in the refrigerator last night,' Grandma told him.

'But Mother,' protested Mrs Bagthorpe, 'surely now that we have achieved our object – and I do congratulate you, everybody, I think it quite wonderful – surely now we can retire, and drink the champagne where it is dry?'

Grandma drew herself up.

'Achieved our objective?' she repeated. 'Laura, after all these years, you evidently do not yet understand me.'

'But surely,' faltered Mrs Bagthorpe, 'you have now established a world record?'

'What we have done,' Grandma corrected her, 'has been child's play. We have merely toppled the record of those trumpery Deanery people. Daisy and I are not satisfied with such half measures. The real work will now begin.'

'The Great Bagthorpe Daisy Chain,' exclaimed Jack, seeing what she was getting at. She was going to set up a Daisy Chain that nobody would ever beat.

'We've got millions of daisies left,' cried Rosie.

'And there will be further supplies growing all summer,' said Mr Bagthorpe gloomily to himself.

William and Mrs Fosdyke advanced slowly through the pouring rain, bearing trays of glasses.

'The champagne, Henry!' Grandma ordered.

Mr Bagthorpe set to work with his thumbs.

'We shall work far into the night,' Grandma told everyone. 'And this time you, Henry, will assist us.'

Mr Bagthorpe was beaten, and knew it. He took his own glass of champagne and went and sat on a waterproof, the rain dripping off his eyebrows.

'The toast, Henry,' said Grandma relentlessly.

Mr Bagthorpe struggled back to his feet. He raised his glass.

'The Great Bagthorpe Daisy Chain!' he croaked.

'And its instigators, of course,' added Grandma, draining her own glass.

She had had, as always, the last word.

Other Puffins by Helen Cresswell

ORDINARY JACK

ABSOLUTE ZERO

THE NIGHT-WATCHMEN

UP THE PIER

THE WINTER OF THE BIRDS

THE PIEMAKERS

THE BEACHCOMBERS

and for younger readers

BUTTERFLY CHASE

A GIFT FROM WINKLESEA

Heard about the Puffin Club?

. . . it's a way of finding out more about Puffin books and authors, of winning prizes (in competitions), sharing jokes, a secret code, and perhaps seeing your name in print! When you join you get a copy of our magazine, *Puffin Post*, sent to you four times a year, a badge and a membership book.
For details of subscription and an application form, send a stamped addressed envelope to:

The Puffin Club Dept A
Penguin Books Limited
Bath Road
Harmondsworth
Middlesex UB7 ODA

and if you live in Australia, please write to:

The Australian Puffin Club
Penguin Books Australia Limited
P.O. Box 257
Ringwood
Victoria 3134